**"I hate a man's touch,"
D'Arcy snarled, "so keep your
pawing hands to yourself."**

"Pawing hands?" Keele asked. "Lady, you don't know what you're talking about."

Suddenly D'Arcy was smothering. Her mouth opened and he was possessing it, his tongue like a brand. She felt a curling sensation in her stomach, a tingling on the back of her calves, as the heat built in her. . . .

"No," she whispered, even as she helped him remove her clothes.

"Yes, my little darling, yes," he said. "Tonight you're going to have a man make love to you. Tonight you'll be a woman. . . ."

Dear Reader:

We've had thousands of wonderful surprises at SECOND CHANCE AT LOVE since we launched the line in June 1981.

We knew we were going to have to work hard to bring you the six best romances we could each month. We knew we were working with a talented, caring group of authors. But we *didn't* know we were going to receive such a warm and generous response from readers. So the thousands of wonderful surprises are in the form of letters from readers like you who've been kind with your praise, constructive and helpful with your suggestions. We read each letter...and take it seriously.

It's been a thrill to "meet" our readers, to discover that the people who read SECOND CHANCE AT LOVE novels and write to us about them are so remarkable. Our romances can only get better and better as we learn more and more about you, the reader, and what you like to read.

So, I hope you will continue to enjoy SECOND CHANCE AT LOVE and, if you haven't written to us before, please feel free to do so. If you have written, keep in touch.

With every good wish,

Sincerely,

Carolyn Nichols

Carolyn Nichols
SECOND CHANCE AT LOVE
The Berkley/Jove Publishing Group
200 Madison Avenue
New York, New York 10016

P.S. Because your opinions *are* so important to us, I urge you to fill out and return the questionnaire in the back of this book.

FROM THE TORRID PAST
ANN CRISTY

**SECOND CHANCE AT LOVE
BOOK**

Chapter

1

D'ARCY KINCAID LOOKED around her, still bemused and delighted to find herself in Greece. She leaned on the railing of the ferryboat carrying her to the island of Keros and tried to absorb all the sights and the sounds around her. Last night she had spent in Athens and although one night in that city could never be enough, she managed to see the Acropolis and the Erectheum. She promised herself that when she was through with this assignment she would take a few days to explore the beautiful city further before she returned to New York and her home. Home. That made her think of Sean and the only cloud there had been on this dream job, leaving him behind with Henry and Adelaide. Sean, at four years old, was a little man with his brown curling hair and tawny colored eyes with the deep brown ringing the unusually light irises. Sean of the stocky, sturdy body, large hands and feet for his age, who was the whole world to his mother, though he was the picture that his father must have been

1

at that age. His father. D'Arcy moved restlessly against the rail, not wanting to think of Keele Petrakis. She had dreamed of him last night. That was disturbing enough. She would not think of him today. She tried to concentrate on a small flotilla of fishing boats on the port side of the ferry, but Keele's face kept intruding, at least the face he had had five years before. She hadn't seen him since the day of Rudy's funeral five years ago. She had left London the next day, flying to New York to Henry and Adelaide and safety. No, no she wouldn't think of the past, not when she was here basking in the hot Greek sunshine on her way to interview Anna Davos, the Greek matriarch who subtly and capably managed Apollo Shipping and Venus Airlines. She was not a woman who had given many interviews, but because of her money and prestige she was still an intriguing figure to the people who read *DAY* magazine. D'Arcy realized what a plum of an assignment she had. Though she could never wish her colleague, Lena Plantz, bad fortune, she had been elated that Gregson Timms, the editor, had to send her in Lena's place when the other woman fell getting out of a cab and sprained her ankle. Since Madame Davos refused to have a man interview her, the job had fallen to D'Arcy, a junior member of the staff even though she had had a few good bylines in the magazine.

D'Arcy thought again how Sean would have loved to see the fishing boats and ride on the ferry. She sighed, missing her son.

What would Keele do if ever he realized he had a son? That thought had plagued her the first year and a half she had spent in the States, but gradually she had come to realize he would never look for her...much less suppose she would have a son by him. To him she had just been a one night stand, one of many in the playboy social life of the ruthless business tycoon, Keele Petrakis.

D'Arcy paced the deck of the slowly moving ferry, knowing that she had another four hours on board and that she would be a captive to her traitorous mind. She was in Greece. Keele was Greek, at least half Greek. The other half of him was heir to Keele Industries, of which he was Managing Director, both in Britain, the parent office, and in Canada and Australia, the subsidiaries. With shaking hand she pressed her forehead, beaded in moisture not just from the sun but from the heat of her memories, memories that she had successfully buried until she landed in Athens yesterday. Why had that started her thinking of him? It had all happened in London, not in Greece. With a groan, she sank into a disreputable deck chair as her mind flooded with yesterday.

She and Rudy Alessio had met as undergraduate students at Hofstra University. Her guardians, her father's brother Henry Kincaid and his wife Adelaide, had not liked Rudy, dubbing him mercurial and unpredictable though they conceded he was quite bright. D'Arcy had been a very young and immature twenty-one to Rudy's twenty-two when they had graduated from Hofstra. Perhaps she would have gone on to law school as Henry wanted her to if Rudy hadn't received a fellowship to Cambridge. He urged D'Arcy to marry him and go with him for the two year span in England. Overriding all objections, she married Rudy and they went to England.

D'Arcy covered her face with her hands as she remembered the early disillusionment with her husband, his bitter denunciation of her frigidity when she recoiled from his rough handling. She learned quickly that Rudy's love was a passing thing—if it had every really existed. More than once he had struck her, so that she had come to treat him with caution, to move warily, making sure that she did nothing to ignite his ferocious temper. Her knowledge that there were other women barely penetrated the cocoon of misery she called marriage. It was a relief when he gave tacit approval to her taking a course in photography. What was first a panacea became an absorbing interest. She and Rudy were almost leading separate lives eight months after their marriage.

It was hardly of interest to her when Rudy gave up his fellowship and took a job with Keele Industries. But when D'Arcy suggested that she go back to the States and seek a divorce, Rudy was furious, disclosing that one of the reasons he had got the job was because he was married. She had to stay, at least until he settled on someone else, he had said, and laughed nastily. D'Arcy had the depressed feeling that Rudy wouldn't find someone else. He enjoyed his freewheeling life with the fast crowd he'd found in London. D'Arcy worked harder and harder at her photography and took part-time assignments with a small newspaper run by one of the teachers of the course.

One evening, Rudy announced there was going to be a company party, the "brass" would be there, and she had to accompany him. "See if you can fix yourself up a little, D'Arce. Your hair looks awful. Too bad you're so tall. I like women small and blond, not leggy and red-haired. Did you always have those freckles on your nose? God, maybe it's just as well you can't have kids. They might look like you. . . ." Rudy's harsh laugh had a bite to it. D'Arcy knew it was because she no longer rose to the bait and fought back, that she just stared at him until his tirade was through. Of course, if he had a few drinks that didn't always save her from his hands, but she had also discovered his cowardice. He was more likely to back down if she didn't. Her first feeling was not to go, but then she discussed it with her friend and mentor, Harold Joyce. He suggested she take a few pictures for the fashion section of the paper, that it might help subscriptions if there were pictures on the social page.

"All right, Harold, I'll take a camera and see what happens. If no one objects, I'll take a few pictures. Now tell me about this little dress shop your niece runs." D'Arcy had smiled at the older man. To her surprise, the shop was quite chic and Harold's niece quite knowledgeable on fashion.

"That tall, red-haired look is all the rage and I have just the green pleated silk that will look smashing on you. Oh, don't look so scared. I'm not going to charge you the full price. I'll consider you my model. If anyone asks you where you bought the dress, tell them Amy's. You'll more than pay for the dress if I get the customers I think I will." Amy had stood back and looked at D'Arcy's slim figure in the peach colored undies. "What a figure! You have gorgeous high breasts, slim calves and thighs, small hips. God, you should model full time." She walked around a self-conscious D'Arcy who fidgeted under the other girl's stare. "Your hair. I'm going to send you to a friend of mine for a good cutting."

"But I've never cut my hair," D'Arcy had gulped.

"I know that," Amy had answered dryly. "With all that curl and heaviness you can't see its real beauty. Besides, all you do is pull it back and it doesn't enhance your fine bone structure, those lovely cheekbones, those almond shaped green eyes. You are a knockout, lady, who is totally underplayed. Now we begin." Amy had rubbed her hands together gleefully, making D'Arcy laugh.

The D'Arcy who had looked back at her that evening from the mirror was a stranger. She was dumbfounded. Her hair was now not quite shoulder length and layered so that the burnished color seemed to gleam in the riot of curls all over her head. For the evening, Adele, hairdresser deluxe, had insisted that the back be swept upward and held by a comb, the other curls cascading forward. The watered silk dress was a hunter green that had a tight bodice held by spaghetti straps, with an inverted pleated skirt that looked like a tight sheath, until she moved and it flared softly about her body. She had never had such an haute couture gown. It gave her back a measure of confidence that had become sadly dented in the eight months of her marriage to Rudy. She flexed her toes in the peau de soie slippers. She knew Rudy would be angry that she was wearing such high heels since it made her taller than he, but she loved them and hadn't resisted when Amy insisted she wear the shoes in the matching color of her dress. And she was so relieved that Rudy wouldn't be coming home to get her! He'd told her in his offhand way that he would take his evening clothes with him and dress at work before going on to the hotel with some of his cronies.

"Grab a cab, D'Arce. Don't be late and try not to look like too much of a drag." Rudy had thrown some bills and those words at her before he had left that morning.

She had used the time during the cab ride to bolster her flagging courage. She told herself that she wouldn't let one thing that Rudy said to her spoil her evening. It had been a long time since she had been out to anything as dressy as a dinner dance. In fact it had been a long time since she had been in her husband's company for an evening. She didn't regret the loss of Rudy's company, but she felt a touch of anticipation at the thought of the evening ahead.

Once in the lobby, she had no idea of her destination, knowing that Rudy wouldn't bother to meet her. She decided to follow the swell of people moving down a corridor to a large ballroom. They had almost reached the doors of the ballroom when another door along the hall opened and disgorged a number of people. D'Arcy stepped back to let them precede her. She kept her eyes averted and thought them all passed when a large hand touched her elbow. She looked up, rather far, at a strong planed face, dominated by a nose, hawklike and strong. Leonine eyes narrowed on her, fascinating her by their gold color with the darker brown rim on the irises. His hair was a burnished chestnut, unlike his black eyebrows. His skin was dark, as though he spent long hours in the outdoors. His broad shoulders seemed to stretch the fine material of his black dinner jacket, as did his long legs pressing against the matching silk trousers.

"You look lost. May I help?" The deep timbred voice didn't surprise her, but the frankly inviting look did.

"No, thank you. I'm joining my husband. Perhaps you could tell me if this is the way to the Keele Industries party? My husband works there," she said. She swallowed hard and was angry at her nervousness. She looked away from that piercing stare, deciding the handsome stranger wasn't going to answer her. She tried to pull away from the hand holding her elbow.

"Yes, this is the way. I'm going there myself. So, you're married to someone who works for the firm? Perhaps I know him." The tall dark man with the large body moved like a cat, his graceful movements belying his strength.

D'Arcy couldn't pull free without making a scene so she allowed herself to be led toward the room where the sounds of conviviality were increasing in volume. "I doubt if you know my husband unless you work in his department. He's a new employee," D'Arcy replied stiffly, trying to keep as much distance as possible between her and the determined stranger. She looked up once, angry at his peremptory manner, to find those leonine eyes, laced with amusement, staring straight down into hers. It felt strange and weakening to look up at a man when she was generally at eye level. She had the feeling she was being dominated both mentally and physically.

"Tell me your name," he ordered softly, guiding her

through the doorway into mass confusion. One hand pressed the small of her back when she hesitated, unwilling to face the milling throng.

"D'Arcy Alessio," she whispered, her eyes darting from face to face looking for Rudy. She hardly noticed the sudden cessation of noise, the growing murmur that was replacing the laughter. Then she became aware that people were staring her way. She wondered with a gasp of nervousness if her slip were showing.

Then she saw Rudy making his way toward her, his curling dark hair still looking boyish though his hairline was receding. His face was flushed and there was a light lipstick smear near the corner of his mouth.

D'Arcy's heart sank as she realized he had been drinking a great deal. Rudy had a tendency to be more insulting and surly when he drank. She drew a breath of relief watching his smile widen as he approached.

"Hello, D'Arce. What kind of hot water have you gotten yourself into this time?" Without waiting for her to reply to his slyly amusing question, he turned to the man who was still holding D'Arcy by the elbow. "How do you do, sir? I'm Rudy Alessio and this is my wife, D'Arcy. I haven't been with the organization long so I'm pretty much of an unknown quantity." Rudy smiled with all his teeth, making D'Arcy remember how she had once thought that his smile was the most beautiful in the world. How ironic! She once thought she loved him too. Now she knew that she despised him. A shiver of distaste made her whole body tremble. She felt the man next to her turn to look at her, but she kept her eyes on Rudy. The man dropped his hand from her elbow but didn't move from her side. Rudy was looking back at her now. "How did you manage to meet Mr. Petrakis, D'Arce?" The words were spoken softly, but D'Arcy felt his menace and took a small step backward.

"Mrs. Alessio didn't have time to catch my name,"

Petrakis interjected smoothly, his eyes going from D'Arcy to Rudy and back.

D'Arcy braced herself when Rudy looked at her again, his glance seeming to tell her how stupid she was. She wished desperately that she had stayed at home.

"Perhaps you'll allow me to get your wife and you a drink?" The question was put, but D'Arcy knew that the man called Petrakis had just given them an order.

Rudy accepted quickly, no longer looking at D'Arcy, but gazing around the room to catch the glances of his cronies. Mr. Petrakis had taken her arm again, but she was able to see the diminutive brunette who was pouting at Rudy as he spoke to her in urgent tones. D'Arcy noted, with indifference, how the crowd parted like the Red Sea as they made their way to one of the bars scattered around the perimeter of the ballroom.

"What will you have, Mrs. Alessio?" He leaned toward her, his rich timbred voice making her jump. She watched those deep golden eyes narrow on her, as though he had just taken her apart, section by section, analyzed her, and assembled her again in milliseconds.

She studied the gold-chased studs in his shirt, swallowing to moisten her dry throat. "I'd like a Perrier and lime, please."

Rudy was there behind her, his fingers digging into her side, making her body arch in a defensive position. She watched Mr. Petrakis's eyes narrow even more on her, then flick to Rudy.

"Pay no attention to my wife, Mr. Petrakis. She'll have a gin and lime. I'll have the same." Rudy's tone was hearty, but his pinching fingers were telling her that he didn't like her actions. No doubt he wanted her to fit the mold of his crowd, D'Arcy thought with bitterness.

When the barman inclined his head toward them, Mr. Petrakis ordered one gin and lime, one Perrier and lime, and an Irish for himself. He looked back at Rudy, staring at him for a long moment, then his eyes dropped to the hand that Rudy had on D'Arcy's waist. The hand fell away.

When the drinks came, D'Arcy took hers and stepped to one side, looking down into the liquid, holding it close to her but not drinking. She couldn't help thinking of later tonight when she was alone with Rudy. She wouldn't allow him to hit her again. She didn't know exactly what she was going to do, but she wouldn't let him touch her.

"Mrs. Alessio?" The low voice was at her side.

She turned with a start to find Mr. Petrakis looking down at her, a rather irritated smile on his face. She looked past him to find Rudy but could see him nowhere. "Yes? I'm sorry. I wasn't paying attention."

"I'm fully aware of that," he intoned, sarcasm threading his voice.

"I'm sorry, Mr. Petrakis. Perhaps I'd better find my husband." D'Arcy began moving away from him. A strong hand clamped onto her arm and stilled her.

"Don't go, and for God's sake call me Keele." He spoke in harsh tones, surprising her.

Her eyes widened on him, trying to read the closed look on his hard planed face. His classic Greek good looks were flawed by the hawklike nose and the small scar lifting the corner of his mouth, she thought dispassionately. "My husband will be looking for me, Mr. Petrakis." She tried to speak in a cool voice so that her own mounting temper wouldn't show. She didn't give a damn how offended he would be. She was sick and tired of being pushed around by men.

"Your husband is busy trying to get the typing pool into bed," he said cruelly, watching her swallow painfully.

She turned her back to him, looking for an exit. She wasn't going to stay.

"Wait." He had hold of her arm again in that firm

grip. "We started wrong." He turned her slowly, seemingly unaware of the curious eyes on them or the people who were edging closer to them who wanted either to speak to the director of the firm or listen to what he was saying.

D'Arcy felt an acute embarrassment as she realized that her name was probably flying around the room from mouth to mouth because she was standing with him.

"Look, Mr. Petrakis..."

"Call me Keele...please." He gave her a smile that rocked her, the white teeth flashing in that tanned face, the eyes glittering gold. "We're starting again. Remember?" He put one finger on her lip.

D'Arcy heard the low gasping murmurs around them and moved back from his hand, flags of red in her cheeks. Damn the man, she thought, grinding her teeth. Didn't he realize he was making a spectacle of both of them? Even being with Rudy would have been better than standing here with this man.

"I think everyone is going in to have dinner now," she said, her voice stiff. "I'll have to find my husband." She ignored the flare of temper she could see in his face, his eyes darkening almost to chestnut, his face hardening as he glared. She shivered as she stepped around him, sensing the rage directed at her.

She had no idea how she got to the table or through the meal. She listened to Rudy's silly remarks to the blonde on his right with indifference, intent only on making her escape at the end of the meal.

Rudy insisted that she stay for one dance for appearance's sake, then he shrugged, saying he didn't care if she went home or not. He was staying and since it was a long drive, he might stay overnight with a friend. D'Arcy nodded absently, sure in her mind that he would be staying with the brunette whose eyes followed them continuously as they danced.

"May I cut in?" The vibrant voice burst right through

her bubble of distraction. She tried to shake her head at Rudy, but he was looking up at his superior with an ingratiating smile that told her it would be a wasted effort on her part to protest.

D'Arcy swallowed past the constriction in her throat, feeling birdlike as she whirled around the floor in those strong arms. Like many large men, Keele Petrakis was a good dancer, his movements light and rhythmic. Her head fit under his chin and though she couldn't see over his shoulder, she sensed many eyes on them. A good dancer herself who had had to submit to Rudy's contrived, jerky stepping, she found a rare freedom in letting herself be swept around the room, her body relaxed in response to the beat and the man's firm lead.

"You're not only a beautiful woman, D'Arcy, you dance like an angel," he murmured, his head lowered toward her.

"Thank you. You dance well, too, Mr. Petrakis," she answered, her eyes fixing on the pleats of his shirt that she was sure were handsewn. She tried to figure out just how many hours that hand tucking would take.

"Do I bore you, D'Arcy?" he whispered, a hard thread of amusement in his voice.

She looked up, surprised, then irritated. "If I thought about it at all, I suppose the answer would be no." Her voice was tart.

The music stopped. D'Arcy felt his fingers dig into her before she was released. "You have a cutting tongue, D'Arcy."

She looked away from those lion's eyes, sure they could lance her veins.

Rudy was there with the brunette, staring at her, then at Keele Petrakis. D'Arcy could sense his anger even at a distance. Taking deep breaths, she angled away from both men and headed for the table. Once there, she picked up the camera, turning it in her hands.

"What's this? Are you going to take pictures?" Keele asked at her back, making her jump. She hadn't realized he had followed her.

"Yes, I thought I would, unless you have an objection. I work for the *Vox Urbis* and thought I would take some shots for our society section."

Keele took the camera from her and looked at it. "I have no objections. Would you mind if I took one of you first?"

"What? But I . . . all right take one." She felt annoyed but managed to smile into the lens. Before she could take it from him, he had turned to someone passing and asked him to take a picture of them. Before she could do more than gasp, Keele was beside her, his arm around her waist. The man took the picture with D'Arcy looking up at Keele. He was smiling into the lens. She still had the picture five years later.

D'Arcy only took a few more pictures. She was too nervous, feeling Rudy's stare following her. She knew he wouldn't be coming home that night, but she also knew the longer she stayed—and held Keele Petrakis's interest—the more his anger with her would grow. Rudy wouldn't forget. He would find a way to get at her and nothing—including all her promises to herself that she wouldn't be intimidated by him again—would stop him from trying something nasty.

With a sigh of relief, she left to find her coat, not even bothering to say good night to Rudy.

"Isn't your husband going to see you home?" The silken voice behind her startled her again.

"Do you know you have the most annoying habit of creeping up on people?" Her chin jutted forward, her hand came up in a fist.

"And you're a little spitfire, do you know that?" He laughed when she sputtered at him. "This is your coat?" He lifted the serviceable, lined raincoat with the frayed cuffs from her hands. "You should have saved a little money on that gown and bought yourself a warm coat."

"Not that it's any of your business, but I was wearing this dress as an advertisement. It doesn't belong to me. So keep your observations to yourself," D'Arcy was stung into replying, well aware of the shortcomings of her wardrobe.

"Your husband seems to dress well enough. Tell him you want more money for clothes," he drawled as she pulled away from him, tying the belt which had long ago lost its buckle.

She wanted to scream at him that she had had the coat all through college, that she was too proud to ask her uncle for money, that her husband gave her just enough for food, that someday she would make enough on her photography to outfit herself. She said nothing, her lips tightening.

"I'll take you home, D'Arcy."

She stopped dead in the corridor leading to the lobby. "No thank you."

"I'm taking you home." His voice was flat.

All at once she felt a big knot loosen inside her. She felt a dike give way on her emotions. "Don't...be... kind...to...me," D'Arcy gasped, her throat working in spasmodic rejection of the collapse. A torrent ran from her eyes, a massing flood that began to crumble all her bastions and she didn't even know why. "Oh God, now look what...what you've done," she hiccuped, dabbing a tissue at her eyes.

He led her from the building, not saying another word.

She was hardly aware of entering the car, its sleek silver interior enclosing her in cushioned comfort.

The car growled and snarled its way through the rain, the headlights and horns of passing vehicles a Daliesque backdrop. The underground garage was quiet after the noise of the street. D'Arcy didn't question anything until they were about to enter an elevator.

"Where are we?" she asked in dull curiosity.

"My apartment. You are in no condition to be alone and that swine you married doesn't give a damn about you."

"I know that," she replied testily, sniffing into the fine linen handkerchief he had pressed into her hand while they were driving. "I want to go home. I can't stay here."

"I'll take you home after you've had a little cognac and coffee."

"I don't drink." She glared at him as he held the elevator so that she could step from it right into the foyer of his apartment.

"So I remember," he answered, amusement in his voice as he lifted the coat from her shoulders. "This is medicinal."

"Baloney," she said, rubbing her arms with cold hands as she moved toward the fireplace that Petrakis had just set a match to. "I like a real fire, not those electric things," she said trying to keep her teeth from chattering.

"So do I. That's why I have one. Here." He spoke just behind her so that when she turned she was standing with her head next to his chin.

When she would have stepped back, he caught her arm, chuckling. "Why are you laughing at me?" She glared from the snifter to him and back again.

"Perhaps at your preference for stepping into the fire rather than being close to me."

"Not much of a choice, is it?" Her voice sounded surly to her ears.

Those leonine eyes had a yellow sky look, storm ahead. "As I've said before, you have a nasty tongue."

"Sorry. You should have taken me straight home. I don't feel like partying." Her voice took on a grating tone. "I think I've had enough."

"Why did you marry that swine?" He tipped some cognac into his mouth, watching her.

"I didn't think he was a swine then." She swallowed a gulp of cognac and her eyes started to water. Her voice was hoarse. "I didn't think I was a homely, frigid bitch then either." She gasped in horror at what she'd said and turned away from him to set the snifter on a carved oaken table that had an authentic medieval look. "I must go home. I'll take a cab."

"No." Petrakis pulled her back against him. "So you're willing to accept his assessment of you, are you?" His voice was rough, but the fingers at her waist were gentle, massaging.

"Yes." The words burst from her. "Because he's right. I hate sex." She pushed at his fingers, pulling them from her waist, then turned to face him. "I hate a man's touch," she snarled. "So he's right." She gulped. "And keep your pawing hands to yourself."

"Pawing hands?" His tones were silken. "Lady, you don't know what you're talking about." He bit the words in half as though they were steel shards. He reached for her again.

D'Arcy had no conscious wish. Her hand flew up and she struck him full on the face. She turned to run, but his hands vised at her hips, lifting her around to him.

His mouth battered hers. She felt as though her lips were split grapes. Panic made her struggle harder, inciting him to tighten his hold. His one hand gripped her neck, forcing her head immobile. His other hand clutched her hips, grinding them into his body.

She was smothering. Her mouth opened and he was there, possessing hers, his tongue like a brand. She felt a weird curling sensation in her stomach, a tingling on the back of her calves, a trembling in her forearms. For one hysterical moment she wondered if she could be having a stroke. Then a heat built in her and her raking fingers clenched on him.

Rudy's face, swollen and malevolent, projected itself on the front of her mind.

"No. Stop. I won't let you hit me. Stop!" Then she choked, hearing her own breathing like the sound of a waterfall in her ears. She only knew that she had to protect herself, that she wouldn't allow herself to be hit again.

"D'Arcy, stop it. Open your eyes. Now." The voice was soft but insistent. "Alessio doesn't have you, darling. I do. I'm not going to hurt you. I never would."

D'Arcy's lids felt as though they had been glued. When she unstuck them and looked at Keele Petrakis, she felt a mixture of fear and relief. "I should go."

"No. I'm not going to let you go." He kept his arms around her as he guided her to the settee. He lifted her cognac from the table and teased her lips with the glass. "Drink this, D'Arcy. You won't get drunk, but you will begin to feel warm and relaxed."

"Why are you taking care of me?" D'Arcy's lip trembled and she bit down hard on it.

"I don't know." Petrakis's face didn't soften. "But I know someone should have been taking care of you for a long time. Leave him, D'Arcy."

She nodded. "As soon as I have enough money for the passage home, I will."

"Where's home?" His voice was gentle as he urged another sip of cognac on her.

"America." She sat back against the welcoming fullness of the couch, the muscles in her neck unknotting a bit.

"America is a big place," Keele said, amusement threading his voice, settling himself beside her.

"Yes, isn't it." D'Arcy's mouth lifted at the corners. She sighed. "It's nice here." She let her eyes rest on the green and cream of the Kerman carpet. "These are expensive." She gestured with the snifter, sloshing some of the liquid up the sides of the glass, and then giggled, leaning her head back.

"Are you drunk on two sips of cognac?" Keele brushed

the corner of her mouth with his lips.

"Four sips of cognac and certainly not." She tried to focus on those leonine eyes so close to her own. "I drank beer in college all the time. I was hardly ever tipsy." She looked at him unsmiling for a moment. "I'm sober. It's just that I feel so silly, so carefree, so relaxed." She smiled again, lifting her free hand and rubbing it along his jawbone. "You should be a psychologist, not a business executive, Mr. Petrakis."

"Call me Keele. I want to hear you say my name."

"Keele." She gasped when his head lowered and his mouth caught hold of hers. The kiss was gentle, persuasive. His body leaned against hers with sensual heaviness. She struggled to keep her equilibrium. "I'll . . . I'll bet you have to shave twice a day."

He ran a hand over his chin. "Am I scratching you, D'Arcy?"

She knew she should say yes, that getting him to shave would be the perfect ploy. Then she could leave when he went to take care of the shadow on his face. "I've felt worse." She stroked his chin, then down his neck. "Do you shave twice a day?"

"Yes." His voice was hoarse as he turned his face into her palm, his tongue tracing the lines in her hand.

She felt her calves turn to water, the fine hairs on her body lifting and being drawn in his direction. She opened her mouth to tell him that she was leaving. Instead she watched him lift her cognac snifter to his lips, drinking at the spot where she had drunk.

"I want you to be my food and drink, D'Arcy." His eyes melted over her. "Will you let me drink from you?"

She looked at him mutely as he pushed her back against the cushions and lay beside her. His mouth was everywhere on her face. D'Arcy had the feeling that he had kissed every pore. His tongue trailed down her ear, his uneven breathing acting on her like a stimulant. Her hands pulled and tugged at the hair that edged his nape.

Never did she realize that touching someone's hair could be so erotic. Her hands seemed to have a life of their own as they feathered his neck and face, then loosened his tie.

"Lady, you are pulling me apart," Keele growled into her neck. "You had better know what you are doing because I know what I'm going to do."

The giddy feeling she had was Keele lifting her into his arms, not releasing her mouth as he mounted the stairs two at a time.

"No," she whispered, even as she helped him take off her clothes. She watched dumbfounded as he rolled her panty hose from her legs and then kissed each knee.

"Yes, my little darling, yes. Tonight you're going to have a man make love to you. Tonight you'll be a woman."

Any answer D'Arcy might have made was lost in his mouth. Then as the heat built in her body, she began to caress him. She was sure that pain would be the culmination of this, but for the moment she reveled in skin touching skin, legs and arms entwined. When she was sure he would enter her she stiffened, at first with the anticipation of pain, then with the suprise that he was just beginning to minister to her with his tongue and hands. It amazed her that the gasps and moans she heard were her own.

When his body joined hers, her delight increased until the bud of feeling burst forth and she felt herself explode in a riot of color.

Keele let her sleep for a while, then woke her again, and the same spiraling climb to sensual pleasure enfolded her. He never seemed to tire of the love play. As she watched those warm, golden eyes, D'Arcy thought she saw a question there, but she couldn't be sure. She was too bemused to try and wriggle herself free of the love cocoon to make sure.

The third time he woke her she went to him eagerly,

caressing him in a frenzied way, as though she knew she had to lose him. Her aggression drove him wild and he cried out her name again and again, his pleasure making hers tenfold.

When he fell into a deep sleep, wrapping his body around her, D'Arcy stayed awake, wanting to savor the moments with the man she knew she loved. Whatever she had felt for Rudy had been a pale imitation of what she felt for this man, this man she couldn't have.

D'Arcy eased away from him when he was breathing in the heavy rhythm of deep sleep. She dressed and left the flat as the gray sky was lightening to a whitish blue.

Rudy was not in when she got home. She took a bath, straightened up the apartment, then set about the task of developing the film she had shot at the party. She went to the office and when Harold said that Keele was on the phone, she told him to say she wasn't there.

That night he called again, but D'Arcy wouldn't speak to him. Late that night the police came and said that Rudy's car had overturned on the M 1, that he and the brunette woman with him had died at once.

Rudy had been an orphan, so D'Arcy had arranged to have him buried in England. She saw Keele at the graveside. She left the next day for New York, unaware that she was pregnant with Keele's child.

Chapter

2

"KYRIA? WE WILL be landing at Keros soon. I have brought you some coffee." The smiling thin-faced young man bowed and left. If he had noticed the shaking of the foreign woman's hand he had been too polite to mention it.

D'Arcy sighed, remembering how Henry and Adelaide had not questioned when D'Arcy had insisted on naming her baby Sean Henry Kincaid after her father and her uncle. She remembered how they had taken the child to their hearts, how they encouraged D'Arcy to seek a career in photography, how often Adelaide had cared for Sean until he was old enough for nursery school. Most of all, she thought of her son with the deep brown hair and the tawny eyes and the chin that jutted out whenever he was scared or hurt. Not that he would cry much. Oh no, even at four he had a crusty courage that would make him tough it out, much to his mother's amused pride. For the first time in a long while she feared that Keele

21

might discover his son. His son was so like him, there would be no denying it, and Greece was closer to London than Long Island. She sipped the black-as-death Greek coffee and pushed the morbid idea from her mind.

Landing at Keros was an event, D'Arcy thought, chuckling as she watched some goats debark in the care of a grizzled man, fully aware that she was not considered as important as the goats to the men on the boat.

A squarely built man with a blocklike bald head approached her. "You are Kyria Plantz?" he asked in heavy accented English, his lips barely moving, his eyes ranging over her with ill-concealed insolence.

"No, I am Kyria Kincaid. Kyria Plantz was taken ill. Perhaps my editor was able to..."

"I am to escort Kyria Plantz, no one else." His body seemed to take on menace.

"Now look, I have my credentials. Just take me to Madame Davos and I will explain to her." D'Arcy spoke in forceful accents but it surprised her when he capitulated. She heaved a sigh of relief, having pictured herself stranded on the teeming dock with nowhere to go but back to Athens.

She followed him to an ancient Rolls-Royce that was in mint condition. It was like sitting in a living room to ride in the back seat.

The road curved away from the dock area and out into the rocky countryside where goats and children roamed the hills. She frowned at the sight of battered donkeys, heads hanging in the burning heat. She had been told that Greeks could be most cavalier in their treatment of animals and not to interfere.

"I'm telling you now, D'Arcy, leave well enough alone. Don't crusade in Greece or they'll toss you outta there," Gregson had admonished her.

The road wound through rock strewn hills, then angled back toward the sea. The house was like a white pearl in green velvet, the lawns leading downward toward a rocky cliff that ended at a white beach. D'Arcy hoped she would have a chance to swim in that clear water.

The heat hit like a hot fist after the air conditioning of the car. Blowing upward she tried to lift the damp hair from her forehead, but her hair had already tightened into more curl. She followed the taciturn driver into the house, carrying her camera bag, the film bags, and assorted equipment. He managed her bags easily and, unlike her, without perspiring.

The front door was opened by a dragon of a woman, black hair going gray, scraped back into a bun. Her highly starched apron crackled and D'Arcy thought even the sound was disapproving. "Miklos tells us from the radio that you are not the right person. Madame may not let you stay." With that she turned on her heel and led D'Arcy across the black and white marbled foyer that was at least two stories high and had a priceless crystal chandelier hanging from its center. The stairway curved in a half circle up one wall, to an open balcony that followed halfway around the foyer.

D'Arcy looked down to see the pursed-lipped dragon holding open a mahogany carved door. She entered a large airy room with floor-to-ceiling windows now open to catch the sea breeze. The room was done in sea green and cream, with matching cushions on the couches and chairs and carved mahogany furniture everywhere. It was cluttered but warm and inviting, understated yet not formal.

The woman who rose to her feet was diminutive, her piercing eyes belying the dainty bone structure. She too had black hair going gray pulled back in a bun. Her dress was black but of the finest silk, her shoes were plain and black but of a soft supple leather. She inclined her head, yet didn't offer her hand. After some moments of studying D'Arcy, she spoke, her voice oddly harsh. "My staff

thinks I should drive you from the island, Miss...
er...Kincaid." The voice was unaccented.

"I'm sorry my editor didn't reach you, but I am qual-
ified to interview you, Madame, and I have all my credentials right here." D'Arcy reached into her shoulder
bag after setting down her camera equipment and prof-
fered the papers.

Reluctantly the woman took them, scanned them, then
gave a minute shrug. "All right you may stay, but if I
decide that you are not what I want, you will go and
there will be no interview. Is that understood? Sit down,
Miss Kincaid, we will have coffee and you will tell me
about yourself."

D'Arcy took a deep breath, throwing a quick glance
around the room to see if the redoubtable Miklos was
poised to throw her out the door. Her first answers to
Madame were stilted and fragmented as she struggled to
keep her composure.

Madame Davos fired question after question, making
D'Arcy feel as though she were the one to be interviewed.
By the time Madame rose, signaling the end of the meeting, D'Arcy's hands were slick with moisture and the
inside of her mouth was bone dry.

"Dinner will be at eight o'clock, Miss...ah Mrs.
Kincaid. You should have told me that you were married..."—Madame looked disapproving—"...rather
than let me find out when you tell me that you have a
son. In Greece we are proud of family life."

"We are proud of family life in my country as well,
Madame Davos." D'Arcy lifted her chin.

The older woman shrugged and turned away. D'Arcy
was sure that she didn't believe her.

She exhaled deeply as she closed the mahogany door
behind her and stepped into the hall.

Maria, the dragon, stood there like a watch dog, waiting only to catch D'Arcy's eye. Then she tilted her head
toward the stairway.

No words were spoken as D'Arcy was escorted to her room by the grim-faced Maria, but she was too wrung out to care. She felt as though she had gone through a police grilling after answering all Madame's questions. Some of the questions that the older woman had asked about her family were too personal and for that reason she had not divulged to Madame Davos that Kincaid was her maiden name.

Maria opened the door to the room, then to the connecting bathroom.

D'Arcy wanted to ask the woman if, after tonight, she would be expected to take her meals on a tray in her room as she suspected, but the older woman seemed loath to linger, so D'Arcy said nothing.

When she was alone she walked to the floor-to-ceiling windows and looked out over the expanse of lawn. Madame had told her that a nephew would be joining them for dinner and that he, too, would be asking her questions. D'Arcy sighed, wondering what other questions he could ask.

She looked around her at the pale turquoise of the walls and ceiling, then went into the bathroom that echoed the same color in floor-to-ceiling tiles. Even the recessed tub, the shower stall, and vanity were in the same aqua hue.

She indulged herself in a bubble bath in the round tub, feeling like a princess when the bubbles covered her body up to her neck.

When she padded back to her room, she couldn't help but admire the handcrafted carpet in greenish blue, the handloomed bedspread a lovely match.

She stood at the French doors that opened onto a narrow balcony and watched the sea darken, noticing idly that there was a sleek black Ferrari in the drive. Her lip curled with distaste as she thought of the poor people on Keros and the ostentation of the Davos family.

A glance at the time told D'Arcy she would have to

hurry. The dress she picked was a shirtwaist in raw silk, the aqua color a shade lighter than her eyes. The pleats were inverted, giving it a more tailored look until she moved, when the material flared about her shapely legs. Her sandals were straps of whitish green leather. She was an avid Third Avenue shopper in Manhattan and had found both a dressmaker and a shoemaker that were skillful and not too expensive. At the last moment, she slung a small camera over her shoulder and hurried from the room, her heels making a tapping sound on the marble parquet of the first floor foyer.

She hesitated outside the sitting room, taking a deep breath.

"You should not be listening outside the door." Maria remonstrated, startling D'Arcy so much that she almost lost her camera.

"For your information I was not eavesdropping," D'Arcy said, flustered, having the strongest desire to point her tongue at the woman whose lip curled with disapproval. Instead she sailed past her into the room, her momentum carrying her almost to where Madame Davos sat talking to someone D'Arcy assumed was the nephew. The man had his back to her but she could see his head over the high backed chair. For a moment as she looked at the gleaming chestnut hair, there was a roaring in her ears.

She stopped dead as she saw Madame's eyes lift toward her. The man must have seen the look because he rose from his chair and turned toward the door in one easy movement.

The shock that registered in those tawny eyes was echoed in her own, D'Arcy knew, but his was more quickly masked. D'Arcy turned to look at Madame, saw her lips move but didn't know what the other woman said. It took every bit of strength she had not to turn and run from the room, escape the house, fly away at once.

Had she conjured him up because she was thinking of him today?

"Mrs. Kincaid? Are you ill? You are very pale. Have you been drinking the water? Mrs. Kincaid?" Madame's voice was even more harsh.

"What? No, I haven't been drinking the water," D'Arcy answered through waxen lips. "I'm fine." She stood there, hands at her sides, feeling as though she was in a tumbrel cart going to the guillotine.

"Well, then come over here and meet my nephew, Keele Petrakis. He manages all my businesses." Madame said this in an amused alert way as though waiting for a reaction from D'Arcy. None came. Madame frowned, her irritation evident as D'Arcy continued to stand there. "He is my heir and the director of all my firms."

"I see," D'Arcy muttered, her eyes glazed.

Keele Petrakis walked toward her, his hand out-stretched. D'Arcy looked at the hand as though it were a hooded cobra. She had to take a deep breath before she lifted her fingers to touch the tips of his. When she would have drawn away, he grasped her hand and lifted it to his mouth. D'Arcy saw the way Madame's head snapped around to observe this, saw Madame's lips tighten before Keele's broad shoulders blocked her view.

"Look at me, D'Arcy. Look at me." His voice grated like shards of steel.

"No." The sound barely made it through her stiff lips.

"You will look at me." His teeth nipped at the soft skin of her inner wrist.

"What are you doing, Keele? What are you saying to Mrs. Kincaid? Do you know her? Did you know her husband?" The querulous voice turned Keele back to face his aunt.

He pulled D'Arcy with him, his hand now at her waist. He led her to a chair and all but pushed her into it. "Yes, Anna, I know *Mrs. Kincaid* and yes, I knew her husband." He gestured to his aunt to resume her seat, then he sat in a chair near D'Arcy. He took a case from his inner pocket, extracted a cigar, then touched a pencil-slim lighter to the tip.

It surprised D'Arcy to see a slight tremor in the hand holding the lighter. When she looked at his face, it was a mask.

Madame Davos shifted in her chair, her frown more pronounced as she looked again at D'Arcy. "You did not tell me that you knew my nephew. I do not like that." She pushed both hands in a smoothing motion down her lap as though she would thrust D'Arcy from her. "I do not want people around me who dissemble. I think . . ."

Before Madame could continue, Keele blew a stream of smoke into the air. "D'Arcy did not know that I am related to you, Anna. She knows nothing about my family." He turned his head, the chestnut hair catching a glint from the lit candles on the mantel. It was too warm for a fire, but D'Arcy would soon discover that Madame always had candlelight no matter how warm it was. The look on Keele's face held a veiled menace. "As I know nothing about her family. I knew her first husband, not this Kincaid."

D'Arcy opened her mouth to answer when Maria entered the room, her slash of a mouth turned upward in the semblance of a smile, surprising D'Arcy. A very lovely woman accompanied her. To D'Arcy she looked like a magnificent magazine cover. Glossy, slick, touched up to perfection, her black hair was in a flawless coil, her brows black and arched, her skin matte white, the red of her lipstick matching her nails. Shoes, bag, and dress were the same black as her hair.

When Keele rose, took her in his arms, and kissed the pouting upturned mouth, D'Arcy felt as though her insides had been cauterized by a hot poker. His smile was lazy and intimate as he looked down at the woman before turning her toward D'Arcy. "Elena, let me introduce you to the woman who has come to interview Anna. This is D'Arcy Kincaid. D'Arcy, this is Elena Arfos, an old friend of our family."

"Darling, how formal you are!" Elena made a moue. "I feel that I'm closer than that to you." She broke into a spate of Greek that had Keele laughing and Madame Davos tittering in an indulgent way.

D'Arcy squirmed in her chair, certain that they were talking about her. An amused glance from golden eyes confirmed it in her mind.

"D'Arcy doesn't speak Greek, Elena. Speak English, please," he coaxed, putting his arm about the tiny brunette and leading her to a chair.

"D'Arcy?" Elena cooed, draping the folds of her dress before crossing her ankles. "Are you on a first-name basis with employees so quickly, Keele? You never used to be so open with the help." She accepted a glass from his hand, looking into his face.

D'Arcy bristled, wanting to upend the drink on that shining chignon. Before Keele could reply, she responded. "How sweet of you to be so democratic, Miss Arfos, but I assure you that I am not part of the help in this household." She rose to her feet setting down her own glass. "Madame Davos, you have already shown a marked displeasure toward me, but I tell you now, I will not be insulted by anyone, nor in any house. I'm sorry not to get this interview, perhaps someone else will have more luck. I'll leave on the ferry tomorrow. Good night. Thank you for your hospitality. I had always heard about Greek hospitality. Now I've experienced it." She saw two circles of red on Madame's cheeks and D'Arcy was sorry about that. She had not wanted to embarrass Madame, but she had vowed after Rudy's death she would take no abuse, verbal or otherwise, from anyone. She felt it was the only way to protect her son, to show him how to grow straight and strong.

She was through the door and at the bottom of the

stairs when the hand grasped her arm hard.

"Where the hell do you get off speaking like that in my aunt's house?" Keele gritted the angry question through clenched teeth. His eyes shone like just-mined ore.

"Take your hand off me. You're not *my* boss. And you can keep your damned bad mannered family, too," D'Arcy spat at him, trying in vain to pry the fingers from her arm.

"We're bad mannered? That's a laugh," he barked, tightening his grip as she scratched at his wrist. "What the hell do you call that performance in there?" He jerked his head toward the sitting room.

D'Arcy could see Maria standing, arms folded in the entrance hall. "Why don't you tell that creature at the keyhole to get lost and I'll tell you?" D'Arcy all but shouted, glaring at the open-mouthed Maria.

Keele's head swiveled around and rapid Greek was hissed from his lips. Maria looked incensed, but she retreated with an angry swish of skirts and petticoats.

"You or no one else is going to speak to me in that condescending, nasty way. That's what I'm telling you and you can bloody well do your worst if you don't like it," D'Arcy sputtered, feeling the tightness in her throat, but fighting. "I am never going to take that again." She pronounced the words like a lesson in phonics, sounding out each syllable. "I can always find another job, too." She wrenched her arm free, her body heaving as she fought to control herself.

He stared at her, his eyes on a level with hers, because she was standing on the first step. Those golden eyes riveted her as though they entered her brain, picked it, and retreated.

With a shuddering gulp, D'Arcy tried to keep her voice steady. "Tell your aunt that I'm not hungry and I will be out of the house in the morning." She wheeled and ran up the stairs, not stopping until she reached her room. She threw herself on the bed, shoving her face into the pillow, forcing her tears to dry inside. She had not cried since she had lived with Rudy. She wouldn't start now.

She had no idea how long she lay there until the restless sleep took her, but the nightmares were there almost at once.

Rudy came at her, his face outsize, grotesque, the eyes and nose protuberant and mean. She wanted to fight back, but fear kept her immobile as he kept coming down that long dark corridor, kept coming and coming until finally he struck her again and again. She woke as usual bathed in sweat, pink dawn replacing gray night light. She rose, showered and packed, and sat waiting for eight o'clock when she would start her walk to the dock to pick up the ferry at nine-thirty.

The knock at her door startled her.

"Come in."

Maria stepped over the threshold. "The kyrie requests that you join him for breakfast. He asked me to unpack your bags, if you will let me. He say that Madame will join us for lunch and that the interview will begin then." The older woman straightened and looked at D'Arcy for the first time. "I can tell you what Madame Davos likes to eat." The woman stared at D'Arcy, as though she wasn't taking a breath.

D'Arcy released the handle of her camera case and nodded. "Thank you, Maria, I would like to know what Madame's preferences in food are."

The woman inclined her head and gestured for D'Arcy to precede her.

D'Arcy rubbed her hands over her forearms and walked past the woman and down the stairs, feeling Maria close behind her.

"The kyrie is waiting on the terrace. I will show you."

She wasn't smiling, but D'Arcy sensed that she had un-
bent somewhat. She couldn't help but wonder what had
been said last night after she had gone to her room.

Keele was sitting at a metal and glass table on a
matching scrollwork metal chair. The terrace was a con-
vex portion of stone and tile that reached out over a lush
garden, giving a view of turquoise sea. The sunlight
glinted on his chestnut hair, showing far more reddish
highlights than she had noticed before. He rose at her
hesitant approach across the tile, his face unsmiling, his
hand going to the chair beside him to pull it back and
usher her into it. "Good morning. You must be hungry,
not having had your dinner last night. I have ordered you
an American breakfast of French toast, sausage, orange
juice, and of course eggs over easy. I'm afraid you will
have to accustom yourself to our coffee."

D'Arcy looked at him, mouth agape. "I never eat
breakfast," she said in fading accents. "I am hungry now,
but I could never eat so much."

"You should eat more. Before you were too thin, too
tense," he growled, though his hand was steady on the
silver coffee pot. "What in hell made you jump into
marriage so quickly after being married to a swine like
Alessio? Don't you learn? Anna says you have a child,
a son." He spit the words from his mouth as though they
were rough stones. "Tell me about them."

"I'm a widow." D'Arcy decided at that moment that
she would volunteer no more information about herself.
It wasn't safe to do so to Keele Petrakis.

His head snapped up and he lowered the silver pot to
the table in slow motion, not taking his eyes from
D'Arcy. "Poor luck all around, isn't it?" His tones were
dry, his eyes flicking over her like a laser, as though he
would disassemble her mind.

"If you say so." D'Arcy cut a small square of French
toast and popped it into her mouth, the taste of the syrup
surprising her. She looked in question at Keele.

"No, it isn't our famous honey. It's maple syrup from your state of New York. I thought you would prefer it."

It irritated D'Arcy to imagine the ease with which he could produce a product no doubt never used in this home until now.

"So tell me about this son of yours," Keele persisted, pushing back the empty plate that he had devoured with the ease of an athlete, which D'Arcy knew him to be.

"Let me finish first." She glared at him. "We can't all bolt our food like a stevedore."

Maria, replacing another silver pot and taking the first, looked scandalized at D'Arcy and even more shocked when Keele laughed. She turned away, her body stiff with disapproval.

"You have shocked Maria by being impolite to the kyrie," Keele observed mildly, swallowing the cauldron-hot coffee as though it were tepid.

"You're the kyrie to her, not to me," D'Arcy snapped, dabbing at a bit of egg yoke that had escaped her mouth.

"You've missed some," Keele observed, leaning forward before she could protest and wiping her chin with his napkin. "Stop glowering at me, D'Arcy. If you want the interview, you'll have to try being civil to me."

"Ha!" She sank back in her chair, holding her cup with two hands, feeling replete and more able to deal with the day. "As civil as your family, perhaps?"

"If anyone is at all insolent to you, tell me." His cold voice sliced across the table. "You should have no trouble."

D'Arcy's curiosity was piqued anew. What was said last night? How was it that Keele wielded so much power in his aunt's home?

"Now tell me about your son. What's his name?"

"His name is Sean," D'Arcy said carefully.

Keele shrugged. "It's a nice name. Goes well with a name like Kincaid. What's he like?"

"Big." D'Arcy smiled as she thought of him. "His

hands and feet are large. He's big boned and he's all boy. He loves animals. He has a dog and a cat. He plays very hard, but even at four he shows a marked compassion for his animals." Her enthusiasm for her son made her forget for a moment that she wanted to be reticent with information.

"Four?" Keele's chair came down on the tile with a crash, the front legs of the metal chair ringing like a bell as they struck. He was lounging no longer, the casual look gone from his face. He was leaning across the table, his teeth bared, a look of distaste on his face as though he had swallowed alum. "What the hell! Did you cross the ocean and jump into bed with the first man you saw?"

D'Arcy cursed her lapse but vowed not to defend herself in any way. She rose to her feet, her hands clenching and unclenching at her sides. "You have no business making remarks about my personal life. My offer to leave still stands," she gulped, as she watched him uncoil his length from the chair, a pulsing threat in every line of his body. She had the greatest desire to close her eyes. It took every ounce of nerve she had not to look away from that graven face.

"You may remain here to get your interview, but stay out of my way. When you see me, walk away, or so help me I'll make you sorry you ever came to Keros." He jumped up and strode off, the violence of the motion tipping back his chair, but he never looked around.

D'Arcy shivered, then eased herself down into her chair. She was sorry already that she had come to Keros! God, it was going to be difficult! She would have to watch every word, every move. She pressed her hand to her throat, feeling the heavy throbbing of the pulse there. Damn the man, he had an awful effect on her. It was a good thing she was so healthy, she thought in silent condemnation, otherwise he might send her blood pressure right through the roof. Probably if she had a stroke on this terrace, he would send a handyman to sweep her into the dust bin!

"You are through?" Maria appeared at her side, making her jump.

"Yes, thank you," D'Arcy said. "And I wish you would make a little noise instead of appearing like a wraith," she told the back of the woman. She looked at the sea, then back at Maria. "Maria, wait. Is it all right to swim from the beach there?" She pointed down the sloping cliff.

"Yes." She shrugged as though the idea were foolish. "It is safe to swim there and it is the private beach of Madame Davos, but we do not have a costume for you. Madame does not swim."

"I have my own suit."

"Then I will get you a bath sheet."

A few minutes later, an elated D'Arcy was wending her way down the curving path to the sea, glad to be free of everyone in the household.

The water was warm as a baby's bath to her toe. Dropping her towel on the sand, D'Arcy sprinted into it, gasping as the water deepened and chilled more. She swam in slow cadence at first, warming up as she had been taught as a girl on her swim team and still did in her daily workouts at the health club. Her pace increased along with her exuberance. She would stop at short intervals to take stock of the distance she had traveled from shore, always aware of not overtiring herself. At one of these stops, as she treaded water and looked around her, she spotted a fast inboard boat curving her way with a laughing water skier behind it.

She had no trouble recognizing the skier—that build and glistening chestnut hair were Keele's. For a moment she reveled in the unaccustomed position of being able to stare at him without being observed. She stiffened when she saw the boat turn toward the shore but felt no

real alarm, sure that the spotter or the driver would see
her. But when the boat kept on coming, she began a
dodge maneuver of her own. Knowing she couldn't out-
run the powerful engine, she beat a path through the
water perpendicular to the boat's, not heading into shore
but paralleling it. Still the boat moved toward her.

She turned her face out of the water to see the skier
gesturing wildly, then she made another turn that pointed
her toward the shore and pulled as hard as she could,
her breathing labored. Unfortunately the boat was now
out of her line of sight and she couldn't be sure it was
not right on her tail. When the sound of the engines
increased to ear splitting level, survival sent her diving
deep. She felt the pulsing roar of the boat and the depth
punishing her ears, exploding her lungs.

She broke the surface in the middle of the boat's wake,
mouth open, gasping for air. Before she could even
stroke, a strong arm was about her.

"I've got you, darling. Relax. I'll take you in." Keele
flipped her on her back, his own voice surprisingly
hoarse. "Are you all right? Were you hit?" he breathed
next to her ear.

D'Arcy shook her head, splashing water into her
mouth. She made no effort to free herself, glad he was
towing her body, now trembling with reaction.

When she felt him stand, she made an effort to do so,
but before she could really try she was swept up close
to his chest, his hands gripping her tight, his face grim.
"I can walk," she whispered.

He looked at her but didn't pause until he reached her
towel, then with one hand he reached down, still not
releasing her. "You've had a shock. You must be kept
warm." He swaddled her like a baby in the voluminous
bath sheet, paying no more attention to her protests than
he did to the diving sea birds that swooped over the beach
and water.

The hail from the boat was ignored by Keele.

"Someone is calling you." D'Arcy cleared her throat. She watched his expression tighten, all the muscles pulling in on themselves so that his face looked etched in slate. His head swiveled toward the boat bobbing near the shoreline. He barked something in Greek and the boat reversed at high speed to race away, wake creaming out behind it.

"Wasn't that your friend, Miss Arfos? Weren't you skiing with her?" D'Arcy asked, trying to get her arms free of the enfolding towel.

"Yes to both questions," he answered, lifting her like a wrapped package and striding toward the cliff face.

"Stop that! Put me down! I can't move like this. Put me down," she sputtered, only her face free of the heavy towel. But it was pressed against his chest, and the curly chestnut hair that arrowed down the middle of his chest tickled her cheek, its soft coarseness like an erotic massage with every movement Keele made.

She remembered how he had looked to her in the lycra briefs as he had rubbed her dry, the black material emphasizing his bronzed skin. She felt her skin heat and was angry with herself. "Put me down at once. You can't possibly carry me up the slope. It's too steep."

"You are heavier than you once were." He smiled, if that grim slash could be called a smile. "There is a great deal about you that has changed." She saw the heavy working of his throat as though he had just tried to swallow a golf ball. "You have had another man. Was he gentler than Alessio? Did you prefer him to me?"

"How dare you ask me that? My personal life is none of your business and I will not answer your impertinent questions," she snapped, feeling those hands tighten on her like a vise.

Maria was open-mouthed, her eyes snapping as Keele strode by her into the villa.

"Get her tub filled, Maria. I want one of the girls to fill it with the essence that Constantia makes for Anna. I am going to give her a massage."

"Not bloody likely," D'Arcy grated into his ear.

"Oh, yes, my little spitfire, I am giving you a massage to get your blood going."

"My blood is going," D'Arcy hissed at him as he allowed her to stand next to the tub now filling with steaming water.

"Maria, let me know when she has her tub. I'll be in the massage room getting my oils together. Tell me if she gives you any trouble." He spun on his heels before D'Arcy could argue.

"Get into the tub, Madame Kincaid. It is better not to interfere with the kyrie when he is in this mood."

"I don't give a cotton damn what kind of mood he is in, if he tries to give me a massage, I'll break his nose," D'Arcy pronounced, her fists clenched.

Maria ignored her, throwing the towel that had been wrapped around her into a hamper. Then she took D'Arcy's arm, helped her take off her suit and slip down into the swirling water redolent of herbs.

When D'Arcy finished her long soak and wash, even letting Maria shampoo her hair, she ignored the woman and the cream colored silken kimono she held out. She sailed into her bedroom intent on dressing.

Keele was sitting on the side of her bed, his arms folded across his chest.

Chapter

3

D'ARCY CROSSED HER arms over her breasts in a vain attempt to cover her nakedness. "Get the hell out of here!"

Keele swung his legs off the bed, not taking his eyes from her for even a fleeting moment. "Stop swearing, D'Arcy."

"That isn't swearing where I come from," she muttered, retreating into the folds of the kimono that a wooden-faced Maria held for her.

"Are you coming quietly or do I carry you?" Keele asked gently, a strange flicker deep in his eyes.

D'Arcy looked at the escaping Maria, then glared at Keele. "You are nothing but a bully. I'm a guest here and . . ."

"Do I carry you?"

"I'll walk."

The massage room was adjacent to a steam room in a section of the house reached by a closed passage. D'Arcy gazed in fascination at the health equipment,

weight machines, full-sized pool, exercise accoutre-
ments. When she started to walk through a door into the
gym, Keele took her arm.

"You can see it all later. First, you're having a massage." As he said this, he lifted her as though she were
doll weight and stretched her kimono-wrapped body on
the table. He looked down at her glowering face, grin-
ning. "You can release your death grip on the kimono,
D'Arcy. When I make love to you, *again,* it will be in
the utmost comfort and privacy, my little dove." He said
this even as he flipped her onto her tummy.

"I'm not little," D'Arcy gasped as those strong hands
pulled the kimono down her back and began to push,
rub, stroke. At first she stayed stiff, then gradually her
delighted body betrayed her and she went limp, her mind
slipping from its mooring and joining her body. She tried
in vain to keep steady, but the effects of the oils and
hands pulled her apart and left her floating. It seemed
she could feel years of strain seeping away, eons of
tension draining out of her, all worry vanishing. After
Rudy's death she had gained some measure of composure, self-confidence, and strength, but being mother to
Sean and holding a full-time job had taken its toll of her.
It seemed to D'Arcy that for the first time in her life she
was being pampered, truly taken care of. She tried to
fight against it, knowing that she would have to maintain
her toughness if she were to survive, that this was only
an interlude and she mustn't succumb to it. That was her
last thought.

"D'Arcy? D'Arcy, I'm through." Keele's voice was
at her ear, tickling it. She was too lazy to lift a finger
and push him away.

"Awright...Lovely...Thank you," she muttered,
not protesting when he scooped her into his arms, liking
the sound of his chuckle as it vibrated against her face,
a face she had pushed into his throat.

"Now you're to sleep for a while," he told her, lowering her into her bed and covering her with the hand-woven spread. "I'll have Maria waken you for dinner."

"Awright." D'Arcy snuggled down into the warmth of the bed, imagining for a moment that she felt Keele kiss her forehead.

When she opened her eyes, Maria was just putting fresh underthings on the chaise lounge near the dressing table. D'Arcy's long skirt of ecru cotton lace and matching off-the-shoulder blouse were hanging on the clothes tree. Maria looked at her, then held her brown strappy sandals in the air.

D'Arcy nodded her head, her sense of well-being so pervasive she didn't want to speak and break the mood. God, she had never felt this relaxed. With a jolt she remembered Keele and his ministrations and she felt a blush suffuse her body. My God, she had acted like a purring Lolita with him. Then her thoughts went further back and she remembered the speedboat coming at her. How had Keele managed to get to her so quickly? He could have been killed! She squirmed in pain at the thought.

"Will you dress now, Madame? Dinner will be soon. Unless you hurry you will be late," Maria said.

D'Arcy dived for the bathroom, giving herself a quick wash. She was about to tell Maria that she needed no help to don the lined skirt that required no slip to rumple its straight effect. Since the blouse was also lined, she rarely wore a bra with it, and her own firm, high breasts were outlined cleanly by the cotton lace lined in cream. She let Maria help her, though, knowing the older woman would not approve that her only undergarment was a pair of bikini briefs. She wore no stockings, liking the feel of her bare feet in the sandals. She added a chunky necklace in coral with matching chunky earrings. She applied makeup sparingly but to good effect, and then stepped back to look at herself. The off-the-shoulder blouse emphasized her long neck, the coral jewelry drew attention to her curly red hair that she had left swinging on her shoulders.

She clicked down the stairs, hurrying, paused at the door to the lounge, took a deep breath, and entered. She saw Madame Davos look up, a tiny frown touching her face for a moment before the usual mask dropped into place. There were two men besides Elena Arfos sitting there. Keele was standing at the teakwood bar. The two men rose at her entrance while Elena Arfos looked at her in cool assessment. D'Arcy didn't so much as glance at Keele, but she knew his eyes were on her. He took quick strides to her side.

"D'Arcy, these are some people I'd like you to meet. This is Elena's father, Gregor Arfos, and this is my plant manager in the States, Steve Linnett. Gentlemen, this is D'Arcy Kincaid from *DAY* magazine. She has come to interview Anna."

Gregor Arfos had a bass voice with a laugh to match. "She should be interviewing you, shouldn't she, Keele?" The laugh rumbled from his mouth.

D'Arcy caught the glare that Anna Davos threw at Arfos and the quick look Keele gave him as well.

Gregor shrugged, then took D'Arcy's hand. "Greeks like that particular shade of red, Miss Kincaid . . ."

"It's Mrs. Kincaid," Keele barked, staring at Arfos's and D'Arcy's clasped hands.

"It's *Ms*. Kincaid," D'Arcy interjected, sensing Keele's head swinging toward her, the sudden menace in him. "I'm happy to meet you, Mr. Arfos." She removed her hand and extended it to the other man. "And I'm pleased to meet you, Mr. Linnett."

"Steve. Please call me Steve. You know we Americans never stand on ceremony with each other." With the carefully phrased sentence, Steve had allied himself with D'Arcy.

She laughed, admiring the maneuver. "True. Please call me D'Arcy."

"Now why haven't I run into you in Manhattan?"

"Maybe eight million others got in the way." D'Arcy laughed again, liking the easy manners of the tall slim man.

"And you must call me Gregor." The voice boomed at her shoulder, making D'Arcy turn.

She caught the flint-eyed look Keele was giving her. He tipped the glass of whiskey down his throat and turned away to refill it.

Elena rose and glided toward them, touching her father's arm with scalpel-like nails colored a rich plum. "Men are so attracted to American women. They are so easy, such party girls I've heard."

Keele's bark of laughter was like a slap to D'Arcy. She could feel her temper heat.

"If you mean that American women can move in any social circle, you are right. We are intelligent enough not to be intimidated by situations that stop lesser women."

Elena's lips peeled back in the semblance of a smile, but before she could answer, her father guffawed.

"American women are quick in every way, eh, daughter?" He gave his barrel laugh again.

Anna Davos rose to her feet. "It is time to eat." She looked at Steve who extended his arm at once.

Before D'Arcy could move, Keele had her arm which he jerked through his own, almost unbalancing her. "Must you be a cave man?" she hissed at him, trying to free her arm.

He didn't answer her or look at anyone. He led her to a seat on his left at the head of the table.

D'Arcy's face burned as she noticed Anna Davos

looking at her with puzzled irritation. The others took their seats in a confused way, making D'Arcy feel that she was not sitting in the seat that had been assigned to her.

She ate the food put in front of her, liking some, finding the meat too strong, the salad delicious. She neither asked for nor offered to take part in the dinner conversation.

"You do not like the lamb?" Keele asked in flat tones.

"No."

"I'll get you something else." He lifted the bell in front of him.

D'Arcy grabbed his arm. "I don't want anything else and if you ring that bell, I'll...I'll throw this wine in your face," she muttered, noting the others were beginning to look their way.

Keele lifted the bell and rang it once, twice, three times, not looking away from her. The glitter in his eyes made her shiver.

She sensed that he would welcome the scene with her, that he would like nothing more than to tangle with her at that moment. A highly developed sense of danger stilled the hand gripping the wineglass. The urge to throw it was almost overpowering, but the violence emanating from him was palpable. She had the feeling that at that moment nothing would have given Keele Petrakis more pleasure than to throw her through a window. She looked down at her plate as Maria scurried into the room.

"Maria, you will bring *Mrs*. Kincaid a steak, broiled medium rare as you have been shown. Do it at once." Keele's voice was like an axe hitting wood. Maria almost ran to the kitchen.

D'Arcy sat there, feeling the dampness in the palms of her hands, looking down at her plate. "I'm not that much of a steak eater either," she muttered, throwing a razor glance at Keele before looking down at her plate again. She could feel four pairs of eyes boring into her.

She fondled the serrated-edged meat knife that lay next to her plate.

"If you try to plunge that into me, D'Arcy, I shall turn you over my knee and paddle you in front of the company." He smiled as he whispered this for her ears alone.

"I've never seen a shark smile before," D'Arcy observed, letting her own mouth widen in response to his.

"Remember that they bite." He grinned at her, his eyes like gold ore.

D'Arcy looked at her plate, anger and embarrassment warring in her as she felt Madame Davos's eyes on her.

The silence at the table seemed to stretch until Gregor Arfos asked Steve Linnett about the business in New York. D'Arcy blessed the gruff Greek's carrying voice that filled the void.

When Maria returned with the pewter platter of steak, the succulent steam wafting around the table. She placed it in front of D'Arcy and conversation died again.

"I regret that I didn't know of your aversion to lamb, Mrs. Kincaid," Madame stated, her words having a hint of frost.

D'Arcy looked down the table at the other woman, moistening her lips to speak, feeling the heat in her face. "Madame, I..."

"Eat your steak, D'Arcy," Keele interrupted, giving her a hard look before glancing toward his aunt. "Of course you didn't know of D'Arcy's aversion to lamb, otherwise you would have ordered the steak for her yourself. Your graciousness as a hostess is well-known," Keele pointed out, lifting his tulip-shaped wineglass and gesturing toward his aunt.

The others also lifted their glasses. D'Arcy saw the momentary tightness of Madame Davos's mouth before she tilted her head toward her nephew, acknowledging his toast.

The moment passed, but D'Arcy was aware of the

others watching her as she tackled the king-sized steak. It was succulent meat but too much for her. She gasped when Keele leaned over and asked for the piece of meat that was on her fork. Rather than create a fuss she gave it to him, glowering. She could hear the suprised murmurs of the others, but she didn't look away from her plate. At last Maria removed the meat platter and D'Arcy sighed with relief.

"Keele, I hope you told Ms. Kincaid how foolish she was to swim out into the boating lanes today," Elena purred.

"Was there a problem with the boat?" Gregor Arfos's bull head swung like a pendulum.

"No problem with the boat," Keele observed dryly. "A little problem with the driver."

Elena pouted. "Now Keele, was it my fault that *Ms*. Kincaid endangered herself?"

"Call her D'Arcy for God's sake," he snapped back. "And yes it was your fault for not taking more care."

Elena looked not the least contrite, shrugging as she stared at Keele. "It is not my fault that she acted stupidly!"

D'Arcy inhaled a deep breath, glaring at the other woman. Before she could say anything, Anna Davos interrupted.

"Tomorrow, Mrs. Kincaid, you and I will begin in the morning. I have decided that I will rise early and then we will be done with this in one day. Does that suit you?" She stared at D'Arcy.

"Interviews are not normally conducted that rapidly." Keele ground his teeth together.

"It is for me to say how long this interview will take. The interview is with me. I wish to be finished tomorrow. Can it be done, Mrs. Kincaid?"

"Yes, it will be difficult, but it can be done, I think. Though it will take the entire day, plus I have to get all the pictures."

"Yes, yes, we will get all the pictures you want. Now I think if we are to get an early start we should get to bed, Mrs. Kincaid." Anna Davos's chin was thrust forward. She didn't look at her nephew as she spoke.

D'Arcy rose, nodding, aware of the churning stillness of Keele. She knew he was watching her as she made her goodnights to the other occupants of the room, but she didn't look at him. Just before she left the room, she muttered a quick goodbye in his direction, then followed Madame Davos.

Maria brought her a cup of steaming Greek coffee a few minutes after seven the next morning, informing her at the same time that she was to breakfast with Madame Davos in her room.

The interview was conducted over breakfast and after, in Madame's bedroom, then in her sitting room. D'Arcy interrupted herself often to take shots of Madame and the villa. Lunch was a quick affair that sat in D'Arcy's stomach like a rock. She was made fully aware that Madame Davos was rushing her away from the island of Keros. Madame had informed her that Keele had left Keros on business and that she herself would arrange for D'Arcy's departure in the early evening.

That night at the hotel in Athens, D'Arcy sat on the bed and reread her notes. It was going to be a good article despite how Madame Davos had rushed her. She climbed into the rather lumpy bed and was asleep almost at once, happy that she would be seeing Sean again, unhappy that she couldn't get the Lion of Keros from her mind. Keele Petrakis had taken hold of her, shaken her from stem to stern, wrung her out and left her feeling like a rag. She would gladly have made a moussaka of him!

The flight home was uneventful. She had found carvings of the Acropolis and wooden soldiers for Sean. She was bringing Henry some ouzo and Adelaide a woven spread.

The weeks following were happy even if she couldn't quite start or end the day without thoughts of Keele. He would crop up in the strangest ways. If a man walked down the street with chestnut hair that had reddish high-lights, D'Arcy would find her breathing impeded. If she saw the back of a very tall man, her eyes would follow him until she was sure it wasn't Keele. It angered her, but she seemed unable to stop.

It was good to be back with Sean. He had had much to tell her of nursery school.

"I'm the biggest, Mommy," he said proudly one day. "And I'm the troll. Jimmy wanted to be but I'm biggest." He smiled toothily, making D'Arcy's heart jerk.

"You're my biggest darling." D'Arcy hugged him, making him laugh even as he squirmed away from her. Sean was getting to the age where he didn't want anyone to think he was too close to his mommy. "Don't you want to hug me?"

"Yes, but don't tell Jimmy, Mommy," Sean solemnly told her while his sticky hands rubbed her cheeks.

She crossed her heart that she would keep the secret. Jimmy would never know.

He raced toward Adelaide's car, hugging his wooden soldiers and talking a blue streak before the car door had closed.

After he left D'Arcy really had to hurry to catch the train. She found that more and more she wanted to spend every moment with Sean and so she left late and had to race to get to the office on time.

Her VW was battered looking but it started on the first try and got her to the station. On the train ride into Manhattan she went over the notes she had made from the letters she had received from Anna Davos. There hadn't been much that Madame had wanted changed from the galleys that had been sent her and the small changes wouldn't be difficult.

She rushed into her little office cubicle, answering the phone as she stuffed her purse into her desk. "Yes? Gregson? Yes, I'll come right away."

She pushed open the door to Gregson's office and stopped dead as Steve Linnett rose from a chair near Gregson's desk. "Hello, Mrs. Kincaid. I was just telling your boss that we've met. That's why I asked that you be the one to do the piece on our firm."

D'Arcy shook his hand, remembering how he'd said they wouldn't stand on the ceremony of last names. But he had just referred to her as "Mrs. Kincaid." "Hello," she replied. "It's nice to see you, but I don't think I have the technical know-how to do a fair job on Keele Industries, Mr. Linnett."

"Sit down, D'Arcy, and never mind the bull." Gregson stabbed the air with his cigar. "If Keele Industries wants you to do it, that's fine with me. Linnett here tells me that one of the main office complexes is right here in Manhattan. Do you know the Athene Building, D'Arcy?"

"Yes, of course, it's just a few blocks away, but I still don't see . . ." D'Arcy began, determined not to take the assignment. Even though Keele was across the ocean, there would be other reminders of him and she was determined to blot him from her mind. Fat chance, a nasty little voice mocked her, when your son is a miniature of him.

"Damned convenient," Gregson growled, waving his cigar at D'Arcy and making her cough. "She'll be glad to do it, Mr. Linnett. She'll be there tomorrow morning. Nice doing business with you." Gregson rose, ushering an amused Steve Linnett from his office and totally ignoring a fuming D'Arcy.

"I know nothing whatsoever about technology," D'Arcy began.

"Not to worry. They aren't. Did a good job for Anna

Davos, so she must have said something to the Keele people. Connection there I think." He harrumphed, sinking back into his chair.

"Keele Petrakis is Anna Davos's nephew," D'Arcy said through clenched jaws.

"That so?" Gregson looked diverted.

"Yes. Now about me doing this . . ."

"You are doing it, D'Arce, starting tomorrow. Just check in every third day or so. Good luck."

"Don't call me D'Arce," she muttered, glaring at Gregson as she retreated out the door. She would have to do it. Gregson saw it as an opportunity not to be missed. She could tell from his bullish look that he wouldn't change his mind.

The next morning, as she stepped from the Long Island train, D'Arcy kept thoughts of Sean in her mind. They stopped her stomach from churning at the idea of remaining at Keele Industries for days, if she were unlucky, perhaps weeks. She smiled as she remembered her son lifting his fire truck into the car, his face creased in determination, shunning any help at all, his tongue protruding from the corner of his mouth. She chuckled to herself as she strolled down Sixth Avenue, hurrying on as two women glared at her suspiciously.

The Athene Building was a fairly new high-rise in glass and stone, poking into the blue sky like a giant harmonica, it metallic-looking windows glistening.

A uniformed guard took her name and consulted his list. Then he pointed to a bank of elevators, telling her to take the far one, a little removed from the others and marked PRIVATE.

She was the only one in the car and there were no stops along the way. When the last light went on, the elevator stopped, making D'Arcy feel that her calves had jumped into her thighs.

She stepped into a chrome and glass foyer. A perfectly

coiffed receptionist smiled and gestured at her to enter the scrolled oak doors to one side of the foyer, also marked PRIVATE. The doors opened at some secret command or hidden signal. D'Arcy had the feeling that she had suddenly gone deaf as she walked through a small inner office where men and women were peering into word processors and computers. Another wraith rose and gestured at another set of scrolled oak doors. She found the mix of chrome and oak pleasing.

A lone woman sat behind an oak desk. She rose, openly studying D'Arcy.

"Mrs. Kincaid? Will you go through that door, please?"

D'Arcy had stiffened at the other woman's assessing look; still bristling she nodded and went through the door. But she stopped on the threshold and stared around her. The room was circular, like a tower room, the windows bowing out in a semicircle of glass. Sunlight streamed in, making the view of New York harbor look like a wraparound mural. D'Arcy hardly noticed when the desk chair that had been facing the windows swiveled around and the man sitting there replaced the phone and rose to his feet.

D'Arcy pulled her eyes from the panorama, her smile fading as she looked at the tall figure framed in the window, his face shadowed but that tall build unmistakable. "You," she croaked. "What are you doing here?"

"I work here," Keele answered dryly. "And this happens to be my company."

"I know that," she snapped. "But what are you doing here? I should be in Steve Linnett's office. Is this it?"

"No, this is mine," Keele answered, a hard amusement on his face as he studied her belligerent glare.

"Then do you mind telling me where Steve's office is?" She spun on her heel, as much to hide the tremor in her hands as to escape.

"You'll be working with me since I know more about my own firm than anyone." Keele's voice was smooth, but D'Arcy had the feeling that his voice was a death knell.

She whipped around to face him. "You can't be serious? You're too busy to bother yourself with an interview. Besides I like Steve and feel we can work together," she said in firm tones, watching the gold ore look in his eye in wary expectation.

"That's the second time you've called him Steve." His tone was silky, but D'Arcy saw the whitened knuckle as he gripped the gold lighter before lighting his slim cigar. "Have you seen Steve since your return to the States?"

"Don't be ridiculous! I saw him yesterday for the first time since leaving Greece," she said, her voice testy as she tried to mask the butterfly feeling that was in all her limbs. She had to get away from this man! "We're Americans. We don't stand on ceremony with one another."

"Did he call you D'Arcy?" His voice was even softer but she had the feeling that she was in the company of the real troll, not the make-believe one that Sean portrayed in nursery school.

"No, not this time, but in Greece we . . ."

"I see. Now you will be working with me so you can call me Keele." His hard smile touched her like a razor.

"You are too busy . . ."

"Will you stop telling me what I can do and can't do? Bossy women annoy me." He leaned over his desk and flicked the ash from his cigar into a gleaming silver ashtray.

D'Arcy moved toward him, clenched fists on her hips. "I am not a bossy woman, but since you feel that way, get someone else." She thrust her chin forward.

When he straightened, he was much closer than

D'Arcy liked, but she didn't want him to see her retreat so she stayed where she was. He reached out one finger and traced her jutting chin. "You are the feistiest female I have ever seen."

"And you have met hundreds of women, no doubt," D'Arcy responded in scathing tones, wishing she couldn't feel his breath on her cheek.

"No doubt." He laughed down at her, making her heart jerk out of rhythm. The man was lethal, D'Arcy thought. He should be bottled and labeled with a skull and crossbones.

She took a deep breath, about to launch into a series of reasons why she would not be on this assignment, when the interoffice buzzer rang.

Keele picked it up, speaking Greek. He broke the connection and turned to D'Arcy. "I'm afraid I'm running late. I'll pick you up this evening..."

"No!" D'Arcy exclaimed, horrified, picturing him seeing Sean. "Perhaps you could find me an office, then I could gather some background. Is there anyone whom I could ask about the things I need?"

His eyes narrowed on her. "I'll arrange something with Gerta. But it won't be Steve." He fired the words at her like missiles before storming from the room.

She looked at the still quivering door and the smooth, sophisticated Gerta, mouth agape, staring in at her. "The bastard," D'Arcy mumbled, not looking at the whispering woman as she explained that she would be glad to show her to an office and provide her with an assistant.

"Ahem... also Mr. Petrakis has informed me that you would find it easier not to commute to your home. We have suites in some of the hotels that you are welcome to use."

D'Arcy's head jerked up. "Yes. Yes, that would be best. I'll arrange to stay in town today. And thank you, Miss..."

"*Mrs.* Olsen," she said pointedly.

D'Arcy felt uncomfortable in the company of Gerta Olsen, who led her to the small area of offices where she would be working. There was another, younger, woman sitting in front of the typewriter as they entered the small outer office.

"This is Mary Marioty, Mrs. Kincaid. She will be assisting you while you are at Athene Ltd." Gerta Olsen showed her eagerness to be quit of D'Arcy as soon as the introductions were completed. She exited at once.

"Isn't she a darling?" Mary Marioty grimaced, making D'Arcy laugh. "I'm Greek, but American born. My husband Miklos was born in Salonika but acts as though he were born here." Mary's impish dark eyes were alight with humor.

The day sped. D'Arcy and Mary lunched at their desks. D'Arcy took time to take pictures of the interior of the Athene Building, which Mary informed her housed not just Keele Industries in the States but all of Athene Enterprises, which included shipping, both air and sea, and diversified electronics interests. D'Arcy was both appalled and impressed at the scope of Keele's empire. Mary made no secret of the fact that it was Keele Petrakis who ran Athene, and not Anna Davos as much of the world thought.

That night in the suite at the Grand Hyatt, after she had unpacked some things she'd purchased, D'Arcy telephoned Long Island again and explained her predicament to Henry and Adelaide more fully. But of course they didn't know the worst past—that she was in the company of Sean's father. Not even to them had she ever told the truth of Sean's paternity, even though she was sure they knew Rudy Alessio was not the father.

"Sean, darling, I'll call you every day. Yes, darling, I'll miss you too. Take care of Adelaide and Henry, yes, and take care of Rag and Mushroom, too. I shouldn't be

more than two days, three at the most. Love you."
D'Arcy swallowed as she replaced the receiver, missing
her son with a hollow ache. He was her life. Nothing
else would ever really matter, she told herself, doubling
up her fists. No other love would interfere...

She jumped to her feet, her white face staring back
at her from the dressing room mirror. Oh God, she still
loved Keele! What a cup of water from a poisoned well
that was! Her insides knotted in nauseous rejection of the
thought. She looked down in a dazed way at the Saks
Fifth Avenue bag clutched in her hand. The triumph she
had felt at charging clothes to Gregson Timms's account
faded away as that realization mushroomed through her
being.

I love Keele Petrakis!

It sang through her mind as she showered and shampooed. It bellowed through her body as she donned the
new peach colored undies she had purchased and the
sheer silklike stockings she pulled over her long legs.
The black silk shirtwaist was so tailored it looked like
an office garment, until she moved and the lighter-than-
air material took on a life of its own, swirling and belling
in graceful rhythm. The dress just reached her knees, so
that her long slim legs were shown to advantage and
enhanced by the peau de soie slings. She carried a coin
purse slung over one shoulder by a black silk ribbon.
Her curling red hair bounced on her shoulders. Her earrings were crescents of jet and jade that curved at the
edge of her lobes. She wore no other jewelry except her
gold watch, which rarely left her arm. She paused for
a moment to look at the decolletage of her dress, toying
with the idea of buttoning up another button, when the
phone rang. She answered and said yes that she was
coming right downstairs.

Keele was waiting for her in the lobby, reading a
newspaper, seemingly oblivious to the glances thrown

his way by the women there. D'Arcy felt like a green knife was slicing her. She couldn't stop watching him.

When he saw her, he straightened up from the pillar he was lounging against and looked at her from head to toe and back again. The smile made her redden and he saw this as he sauntered toward her. The smile deepened. "You look lovely."

Her eyes were pulled to his; the heat she found there ignited her body, making her feel that his liquid eyes had just spilled over her. Taking a breath, she looked around her, surprised to find that people were still moving about them, that the world hadn't stopped, that no one else seemed to have been affected by the upheaval.

"I have reservations for eight-thirty. Shall we go?"

D'Arcy couldn't even speak, couldn't even ask where they were going. She simply allowed him to take her elbow and lead her from the building. The chauffeured limousine waiting at the curb surprised her.

Keele shrugged as she turned to look at him. "It's easier to get around New York at night this way."

"Is it now? I'll have to remember that," D'Arcy said.

Keele laughed. "Don't you know you should sweeten some of that vinegar? Perhaps the champagne will help."

"Champagne? Why are we having champagne?" D'Arcy tried to rally.

"To celebrate," he breathed, moving across the seat.

"Oh? Celebrate what?" D'Arcy looked at him as though he were a hooded cobra.

"Our engagement, of course." Keele's mouth swooped over hers, catching her open-mouthed protest into his own. The sudden invasion of her mouth sent such a wave of weakness through her that she had the frightening feeling she had just overdosed.

Chapter

4

"YOU...ARE...ONE...brick short." D'Arcy gasped, trying in vain to free herself from his hold. "I have never heard such a ridiculous thing in my life. Will you let me go!" She struggled, glaring at his amused face.

"We are becoming engaged tonight, D'Arcy," Keele said, his smile still in place but his eyes hard and determined. "I count myself lucky you haven't jumped into bed with another man as yet."

"You bastard!" she sputtered, trying to push at his shoulder. "Even if I do have a relationship with another man, it is certainly no business of yours. Release me!"

The long fingers bit into her shoulders. "And have you a relationship with another man, D'Arcy? Tell me."

D'Arcy threw back her head, fully intending to tell him yes, she had something going with someone else and that he could go to hell. But those gold ore eyes pierced her through. "No," she said. He shook her. "I mean no, I haven't involved myself with anyone." She

57

swallowed, looking away from him. "Now will you let me go?"

"No, my little D'Arcy, I will never let you go." He folded her close to his side, his mouth sliding down her cheek.

She shivered as unbidden tears clouded her eyes.

"Are you cold, darling?" Keele whispered, his arms tightening.

She shook her head, unable to answer him, her throat filled with unshed tears.

"You'll enjoy it tonight. This show is supposed to be the best comedy to come along in years. Then we're having dinner at a very intimate restaurant I know, then we'll dance. I know you are a beautiful dancer. I thought of that so many times."

D'Arcy peered up into his face, lit by the passing lights of the Manhattan theater district. "I'm sure I'll enjoy tonight, but you must be joking about our engagement. That's impossible."

She felt Keele's whole body harden at her side. "I'm not joking and it's not only possible, it's a fact that you and I are engaged. I have arranged for the announcement to be in the papers tomorrow."

"You what?" D'Arcy jackknifed erect, horror coursing through her. "You can't have done such a thing! What will Henry and Adelaide think. My God, someone will tell Sean."

"You can tell him yourself. I'm giving you tomorrow off to take care of things like that. While you are explaining it to your son, you might tell him that I wish to meet him. Arrange that too. Who are Henry and Adelaide?"

"My aunt and uncle," D'Arcy answered, her voice dazed. "They take care of Sean for me at times."

Keele led her down the theater aisle, keeping a warm hand at her back.

Even in her bemused state, D'Arcy noticed how many people hailed Keele and how many of the women glared at her. D'Arcy was drowning in her own misery, too much to react to the feminine glowers, but not so much that the fact that they existed escaped her.

The comedy was good, their seventh row seats allowing them to catch every nuance. At the intermission, Keele introduced her to several of the obviously envious women and their escorts.

"This is D'Arcy Kincaid, my fiancée and also the woman who is doing the article on Athene Ltd. for *DAY* magazine." Keele smiled at the ohs and ahs, accepting congratulations and best wishes with aplomb.

"Keele, darling, *you* married? I don't believe you will allow that to happen. It might make you boring." A stunning blonde, tiny and sleek, cooed this to him, grasping his arm and staring at D'Arcy with a mixture of disbelief and distaste.

"Is that what happened to you, Mrs. Bolle?" D'Arcy inquired, a smile pinned to her lips.

"I'm divorced, dear," Marianne Bolle responded, not liking it when Keele disentangled himself from her and placed a possessive arm around D'Arcy.

"Come along, Marianne," a man called Hudson said.

"I'm coming. But first I must ask why Keele hasn't given you a ring, dear." Marianne pouted as if sympathetic.

"D'Arcy prefers to choose her ring. We haven't done that yet," Keele said.

"My dear, how silly of you." Marianne pretended shock. "Keele has impeccable taste. I can vouch for that." She whirled away on the arm of her escort, leaving D'Arcy clenching and unclenching her hands.

"I would be grateful if you wouldn't trot out your entire stable of mistresses for me to see." D'Arcy spoke through her teeth as they resumed their seats.

"Oh? What makes you think that Marianne is—or ever was—my mistress?" Keele asked, a glitter in those yellow eyes.

"I'm not that stupid," D'Arcy answered, her tones lofty, wishing he had denied it outright. She wouldn't have believed him, but she wanted the denial anyway. "I'm sure you don't give passing strangers jewelry."

"You're right there," Keele said, then sank low in his seat as the curtain lifted.

Dining was like a trip to Maxime's, D'Arcy thought. A deferential French-speaking waiter informed them of the choice that evening. And the music and entertainment were strictly "Paris!" When D'Arcy mentioned this to Keele, he shrugged and smiled.

"I don't think Marcel would be as flattered as if you had compared his place to a waterfront cafe in Marseille. He is very proud of his home city and when you taste the bouillabaisse you will think you really are in Marseille."

"I wouldn't know. The only city in France I have visited is Paris," she said in a stiff voice. "That's one of the penalties of being middle class, we don't travel on a whim."

Keele steepled his hands in front of him, smiling at D'Arcy, his lips derisive. "And that's another mark against me I'm sure, that I've had enough money to see the world and back again. I also speak five languages and understand quite a few more. I can give you more evidence of my disreputable character, D'Arcy."

Her lips twitched, but she kept her eyes fixed on the clam shell floating in her birdbath-sized bowl. "I don't know how I'll eat all of this. The portions are huge." She spooned some of the liquid into her mouth, letting her eyes close. "It is very, very good."

Keele looked at her. "Changing the subject are we? Good. I didn't relish tying myself to the stake and watching you run for a burning torch."

"Martyr," she murmured, breaking a hot crusty roll.

Keele gave a soft burst of laughter, making her smile. When he sucked in a breath and grasped her hand she was startled. He pressed a kiss into her palm, and she gasped. "No matter what happens, I know I'll never be bored by you, D'Arcy."

When their waiter brought the silver tray banked with pastries, D'Arcy sadly had to shake her head no. She sighed. "I'm a chocaholic, you see," she explained, wincing as she looked at the eclairs and German chocolate cake. "No room."

Keele laughed again and ordered the cheese board for himself and brandy for them both.

When D'Arcy turned the snifter in her hands, the liquor seemed to take on a jewel tone as the candlelight refracted off it. "Keele, I will do this job for you, but I think this joke about an engagement has gone far..."

"It's no joke, D'Arcy. We're getting married," Keele pronounced in measured tones, looking at her over the lip of his snifter. "Don't try to fight me on this. You won't win."

"But why?" she hissed at him, taking a sip of the cognac, then coughing.

"Many reasons. Pick one." Keele shrugged his shoulders.

"You're crazy," she muttered, suddenly feeling a great desire to be married to him, suddenly wishing that she could have a home with him. The thought stunned her and she took another gulp of brandy.

"Didn't anyone ever tell you that you do not gulp forty-year-old cognac?" Keele looked at her, one eyebrow raised.

"Don't tell me what to do," D'Arcy mumbled, feeling the heat of the brandy course through her. Perhaps she could just be engaged to him for a little while. It could be quite lovely. With that satisfying thought she sat back in her chair and smiled at the man sitting opposite her.

And when she leaned forward to take one green grape from the cheese board, Keele grasped her left hand.

She was looking at his face in an inquiring way when she felt the cold metal slipped onto her finger. "But... but you said that I would prefer to choose..." D'Arcy sputtered, looking from Keele's face to the marquise shaped emerald that seemed to dwarf her hand.

"Marianne Bolle is not privileged to know our business. Besides I had that ring made for you. It reminds me of your eyes."

"And it's the same size as one of my eyes too," she mumbled, moving her hand to catch the light. Then something he said penetrated. "You had this made? When?"

Keele shrugged. "It's not hard to get things done."

"Not for you at any rate," she answered tartly, vaguely aware that he hadn't answered her question.

She left the restaurant in a haze, barely aware of the walk they took to Arthur's. The dancing was in full spate. It surprised D'Arcy to notice that some of the celebrities she recognized were not nearly as tall in real life as they seemed to be on the movie screen or on television. Most of them stopped to speak to Keele, who was friendly but not encouraging. When they rose to dance, D'Arcy felt the ghosts of their past, and trembled.

The shudder that shook her made Keele lean back from her. "That wasn't from the cold. What is it, D'Arcy?"

"I was thinking of the night we met," she said through lips gone stiff.

Keele folded her closer, his body bent over her as a shield. "You're remembering Alessio, aren't you?" He felt the nod of her head against his chest. "Don't think of him! He was a bastard! If he hadn't been killed, I think I would have done the job myself. I can still hear your whimpers when I began to make love to you as though you expected me to be the swine that he had been with you."

Heat rose in her body as his lips slid down her cheek. She could almost feel again the awesome joy she had experienced with Keele, those many years ago in London.

She loved Keele Petrakis. She had loved him in London and she loved him still. She was sure there was no way on earth that they could be happy with one another with so much between them, yet she knew with a blinding certainty that there was nothing more on earth that she wanted than to be his wife. She wanted to lie with him and feel that warm, secure river of delight that only he could give her.

"You weren't frightened with me, were you, darling?" His husky question was muttered into her hair.

"No." She tried twice before the simple negative could pass her lips. The breath left her body as his arms tightened on her. It seemed the natural thing to do to lift her face and place her mouth against his neck.

"God, darling, let's get out of here. We'll go to my apartment," Keele growled, his heart thudding under her cheek.

A measure of sanity came back to D'Arcy as he began leading her from the floor. "No," she whispered, her voice thick, fighting to keep her equilibrium. "I . . . we can't. You said we were going to dance, that we were going to celebrate."

"We can celebrate in bed." Keele stared down at her, his eyes liquid and leaping with heat.

"No, don't rush me. I want to break the news to Sean and Henry and Adelaide first." She saw a look of violence in his face, then he seemed to wrestle himself into composure.

"Don't play games with me, D'Arcy. It was pretty strong stuff between us. That hasn't changed. I want you and I want you now." He looked down into her eyes and after a long summing up, he sighed. "All right, you win. Tonight we dance and I take you straight home, but we're getting married, D'Arcy, and soon. I've waited too long as it is." He steered her back to their table and poured Dom Perignon into a glass for her. "To us, my little wildfire, and to our life together, which should be very interesting." He smiled at her, but his eyes had the look of lode ore again.

D'Arcy swallowed and lifted her glass.

They danced into the wee hours. It seemed to her that Keele drank a great deal though it didn't appear to affect him, outside of the glitter that grew in his eyes. Once she caught him staring at her, brooding menace in that look, and she shivered.

When he left her at her door, his kiss was hard and bruising. She tasted blood in the inside of her mouth.

The relief at being alone was so great that her whole body shook with it. She was bone tired but when she did get into bed, her eyes stayed open as though they were frozen.

The next morning when she looked out her window at the New York skyline, the day was as gray as her spirit. Rain slanted against the glass, making her think of tears. She hadn't slept, but she didn't feel tired. She felt as though she were being wheeled into surgery and that the doctor had informed her there would be no anesthesia.

She used more makeup than usual, trying to cover the pallor of her skin.

The early train out to her town was almost empty and she pulled her battered car into the Kincaids' driveway just as Henry was reaching down to pick up the paper from the doorstep.

"D'Arcy! What are you doing here? I thought you were staying in town for a few days."

"I was." She reached up to kiss her uncle before passing him to enter the house.

Sean saw her almost at once and as usual had much to tell her. "I don't have to go to school yet, Mommy. Did you come to kiss me goodbye?"

"Yes, I did, but I also wanted to talk to you before you went to school, love."

She held Sean on her lap and sipped the coffee Adelaide had poured for her. She had a hard time looking at the two persons who were so close to her, aware of their worried gaze. "Sean, you always told me that you would like a father. Isn't that so?"

The little boy nodded, leaning back against her. Then he shot up straight. "Have you found my daddy?"

"I'm going to marry someone who will be your father," D'Arcy announced, her lips waxlike. She heard the surprised sounds coming from Henry and Adelaide.

"Will I like him?" Sean asked, trying to feed a crust of toast to his cat and laughing when the dog took it instead.

"Yes, I think so," D'Arcy answered, hearing the uncertainty in the hollowness of her voice.

"All right then," Sean answered, slipping from her lap and running to the front door. "Jimmy's mommy is here. Where's my lunch?"

The flurry of his departing gave D'Arcy a few moments to pull herself together before Henry and Adelaide followed her back to the sitting room.

Henry cleared his throat. "Now, D'Arcy honey, I don't want you to think I'm prying, but are you sure you know what you're doing?"

"Yes." She smiled, a mere lifting of one side of her mouth. "I know what I'm doing. The man's name is Keele Petrakis and we're engaged. See." She held out the hand with the exquisite emerald, her smile widening as Adelaide gasped. Henry was still frowning.

"You've never mentioned this man to us before, D'Arcy." He pushed tobacco into his pipe, his movements jerky.

"I know. Please trust me. There are some things that I haven't told you, but you must know that I would never do anything that would in any way hurt Sean."

"We know that, dear," Adelaide soothed.

"And how about you? Your happiness is important, too, D'Arcy. Don't just marry a man because Sean needs a father." Henry spoke slowly, his voice brusque.

"I love him." D'Arcy swallowed, the words seeming strange.

Henry let out an explosive sigh. "That's good. I just hope he's good enough for you, my dear. I want you to be happy."

"I know that." D'Arcy couldn't stop the tears from rolling down her cheeks. She welcomed their hugs and murmurings of love, needing their warmth.

"Something is wrong, D'Arcy. I can feel it," Henry said after Adelaide went to the kitchen for the coffee. "Can I help?"

"You are helping me by the way you care for Sean." She sighed and looked away from Henry's concerned gaze. "There is something bothering me, but I'd rather not talk about it now."

"Anything you say, my dear. You know your aunt and I love you as though were were our own."

"I know." D'Arcy's eyes moistened again. "I can never tell you how grateful I am for all you've done for me and for Sean."

"Child, don't you know by now that you brought life into our lives when Sean was born. We love him and I think that he loves us."

D'Arcy nodded, lifting her uncle's hand to her cheek.

On the train returning to Manhattan, she had twinges

of guilt about not telling Henry and Adelaide that Keele was in truth Sean's father. She pressed a hand to her warm face. How could she ever explain that to them! Perhaps they wouldn't notice the resemblance when they met Keele, D'Arcy thought, not with too much hope.

She also felt guilty about leaving Sean for so many days, but she made up her mind that as soon as she had this assignment finished on Athene, she would tell Gregson Timms that she wanted some time off to be with her son. Columbus Day was coming up and Sean would have a long weekend. That would be ideal. Then she thought of what Keele would say about her being on Long Island, The hell with him! She gritted her teeth, knowing the rage he would be in when he found out about Sean being his son. Well, she would have to deal with that when the time came. Somehow, even if he hated her, she would make him listen. She had to make him listen. Depression wrapped her like a cloak.

The next morning when she left her hotel to walk to the Athene Building, the sun was shining. The day looked hand laundered but cold. She was standing at the entrance to the Athene wondering where she should breakfast.

"Good morning, D'Arcy." Keele's mouth swooped to hers.

The tenderness held her immobile before she broke free. "On a public street?" she asked, not looking at him, willing her hand to stop shaking as she pushed it through her hair, ruffled by the light but cold autumn breeze.

"No one even looked," Keele said, amusement threading his voice as he ran one hand down her cheek.

D'Arcy looked through her lashes at the hurrying New Yorkers, not one of them gazing her way. "Even so," she mumbled. "Goodbye, I'm going to eat breakfast."

"How sweet of you to invite me, love," Keele purred, taking her arm and leading her into the foyer of the massive building and nodding to the security man. He pressed the button on the private elevator which opened at once.

"I didn't know you came to work this early," she sputtered, trying to pull away from his hand. "Will you let me go? I told you I haven't eaten yet."

"First, let me tell you my days usually start early. I have major responsibilities, my dove. Second let me tell you that I didn't forget your breakfast, that I called your hotel so that I could pick you up and take you out to feed you. That's what I'm doing now. My secretary will have had someone bring us some food. Of course I would have preferred to pick you up and take you somewhere other than my office...but I'm sure you'll get enough to eat." He smiled and ran the palm of his hand down her derriere. "Not that I want this any more rounded than it is. I don't."

D'Arcy jumped as though she had been scalded. Before she could say anything, the elevator opened to his office and to the large welcoming smile of his receptionist. D'Arcy could do no more than glare at him.

Humor twitched at his mouth and lit his eyes, making D'Arcy reel at the power of the man.

When she walked into his office and looked at the semicircle of windows, her first thought was how clear and uncomplicated the air looked, unlike her own life at the moment.

"I haven't had my kiss yet," Keele said at her shoulder before he spun her around into his arms.

"You did too..." The rest of her words were swallowed into his mouth. She felt the thrust of his tongue and her legs buckled under her.

Without removing his mouth, Keele swept her up into his arms and swung himself down into his leather chair, D'Arcy cradled against him.

There was no struggling against him or herself. He

forced her deeper into his arms, demanding the response that she gave. Her heart felt as though it had leaped through her skin and was joined to the erratic rhythm of his. Her fingers knotted into his hair, trying to bring that head closer.

"Ahem, Mr. Petrakis, your breakfast is here. I tried to ring you, sir. I don't suppose you heard me," the secretary said in a flat voice.

Keele lifted his head, not releasing a gasping D'Arcy. Though his voice was steady and there was a smile on his lips, D'Arcy could hear the thunder of his heart under her face. "I suppose I didn't. Send them in with the food . . . and Gerta . . ." Keele levered himself to his feet, allowing D'Arcy to stand. "You can congratulate me. Mrs. Kincaid has consented to be my wife."

"Congratulations." The business smile turned to D'Arcy. "And best wishes to you, Mrs. Kincaid."

She loves him, D'Arcy thought. Her next thought was that the woman couldn't have him! D'Arcy was appalled at the anger that coursed through her. She wanted to hit the perfectly groomed Mrs. Olsen and roll her in mud.

"Ah, here we are. I hope this is good. My fiancée has an excellent appetite," Keele said to the white-coated attendant.

"How about your own appetite?" D'Arcy shot back, surprised and pleased when Keele threw back his head and roared with laughter, then caught her close to himself, holding her with a casual possessiveness that made the food server smile knowingly.

Mrs. Olsen marched into the office carrying a silver tray, in a ritualistic way that made D'Arcy's teeth come together.

"I'll make the coffee, Mrs. Olsen," she said in firm tones.

Perfectly pencilled brows rose in question as Gerta Olsen looked at her employer, but answered D'Arcy:

"But Mr. Petrakis likes his coffee a certain way."

"I think I can muddle through," D'Arcy said through her teeth.

Keele looked away from the breakfast tray at the sound of her voice. His gaze touched Gerta, then went back to D'Arcy. "My fiancée will make the coffee. Thank you, Gerta. That will be all."

The woman inclined her head toward her employer as he stared at her.

"Come along, darling," Keele said to D'Arcy. "The eggs are just the way you like them." He coaxed her from the coffee pot.

"How do you know how I like them?" she asked, her throat drying at the look in his eyes.

"I remember what Maria told me when I asked her what you like to eat."

"You asked Maria what I liked?" D'Arcy asked, her mouth agape.

"Of course, I wanted to know what kinds of food Maria would have to begin stocking in the house for your visits."

"My visits?" D'Arcy whispered.

"Yes. And dammit, stop repeating everything I say, like some tropical bird."

"I'm not your bird," D'Arcy riposted weakly, making Keele laugh before he crossed the room and took her arm to lead her to the table.

"Yes you are. You're my bird, my fiancée, my wife, my woman. You're all the women in one to me, D'Arcy. Nothing can change that." He put a delicately scented lemon marmalade on a triangle of toast and fed it to her.

Don't bet on it, D'Arcy thought, chewing on the toast and watching him tackle the bacon and eggs in front of him.

"The coffee is good, D'Arcy. Who taught you to make Greek coffee."

"There *are* recipes books," she snapped, feeling the blood run up her cheeks when he chuckled and traced her jawline with one finger.

"So, my dove, you wanted to know how to please me too?" Keele grinned, then put one finger over her lips. "Don't bother denying it. I like the thought of your wanting to please me."

"You won't always be pleased with me, Keele, any more than I'll always be pleased with you," D'Arcy hedged. Suddenly she felt sick. How quick, too quick she'd been to announce to Sean that he would have a father. And when Keele found out the truth of Sean's birth, he might be too furious with her to marry her. She thought she was coming to know this untameable English-Greek she had agreed to marry. He would consider her silence all those years as to her whereabouts and the birth of Sean a blow to his pride, a deep insult. He would not be able to forgive her. D'Arcy moaned inside herself.

"What is it, D'Arcy? Is the coffee too strong for you? You have the look of someone who has something bitter in her mouth."

"Coffee's fine," D'Arcy mumbled around the toast she pushed into her mouth, not able to talk with him at that moment.

Just when they were both finishing, a light on his desk flashed.

"Yes?" Keele answered, nodding. "Yes, I'll take it." He turned from the phone. "Darling, I have to take this call..."

D'Arcy lifted her hand, palm out. "I understand. I'll just go down to my own office. Thanks for the breakfast." She started to leave, when Keele reached out and fastened onto her wrist.

"Not without my kiss." His gold eyes were lava hot as he pulled her round the desk and down to him.

She resisted when the kiss lengthened and he tried to

pull her into his lap. "No, you'll never take your call if I don't leave now."

He released her reluctantly, his eyes narrowing for a moment before he shrugged. "You're right. I'll see you in a little while."

D'Arcy left the office without even looking in Mrs. Olsen's direction, afraid she would poke her tongue at her.

Once at her own desk, she tried to make sense of the notes she had taken but found she could only concentrate on Sean and what steps she would have to take to insure that Keele's temper did not touch him.

She was sitting with her head pressed into her hands, her elbows on the desk, and didn't hear the door open.

"Hey, lady, what's the problem?" Steve's voice penetrated her fog and she lifted her face to stare at him. "D'Arcy, what's wrong?" Steve hunkered down beside her desk, gazing at her with a creased brow.

"It's nothing. I've just been worrying about my son." She tried to smile, but her rubber-stamp lips wouldn't hold the curve.

"I think you're worried about Keele Petrakis, too. I've seen..." Steve paused, as D'Arcy's left hand splayed on the desk and he caught the green glitter on her left hand. "Wow, that's beautiful. Are you engaged to Keele?" His question was a little stiff.

"Yes, at this point I am, but I don't know how permanent it will be."

"Are you worried that Keele won't want your son around?" Steve frowned, curiosity flitting across his face. "If so, I can tell you that he always seemed to be on good terms with his nephews and nieces and his friends' children. I've seen him often with kids around him." Steve lifted one hand to her cheek, his fingers soothing.

"They do say that Greeks love children." D'Arcy tried to smile.

"And so do the English . . . and Keele is English, too. He was born and raised, schooled and formed in England," Steve added, pulling her to her feet and leading her to the window. The antlike people on the street below scurried to and from their holes.

Sighing, D'Arcy leaned her forehead on the cool glass. "Somehow he always seemed pure Greek to me . . . or is it pure womanizer!"

Steve laughed, putting his arm around her. "He is pretty strong stuff where the women are concerned. It isn't all his fault. You should see the women throw themselves at him." Steve leered down at her. "I try to catch his fallout."

D'Arcy looked up at him, not trying to move away from that comforting arm. "Oh, I don't imagine you have too much trouble."

He laughed. "No, but I don't draw the high-powered stuff that Keele does."

"Ahhh, poor baby," D'Arcy said, feeling her spirit lift a little. "And I'm sure that there are only ugly women working at Keele Industries and Athene Ltd."

Again he laughed and D'Arcy chuckled with him. "Have you seen my secretary, D'Arcy? A very ugly woman, indeed! Along the lines of Gerta Olsen," Steve growled, leaning down toward her. He didn't have to lean far since D'Arcy was tall. For a moment their faces were almost touching.

"Am I interrupting?" The cast iron in Keele's voice was cloaked in velvet.

D'Arcy gave a start and whirled to stare at him, open mouthed at the heat leaping in those topaz eyes. The violence came off him like a charge. She had the feeling that the fine hairs on her body were lifting and leaning toward him. She swallowed, tossing words around her mind like spilled gum balls. She had a skin-prickling certainty that the wrong words would catapult him across the room like a missile.

"Steve was telling me about his secretary," D'Arcy said in measured tones.

"Was he?" Keele's voice was still soft. He aimed those eyes at Steve. "Leave."

"Now, Keele..."

"Leave, Linnett, while you can still walk."

Chapter

5

D'ARCY CLENCHED AND unclenched her hands, staring at Keele, anger warring with caution. Anger won. "What's the matter with you? Talking to Steve like you might punch him or something!"

"I meant exactly what I said. I won't tolerate your being with other men, D'Arcy." He fired the words at her like bullets.

"You're crazy," she hissed at him. "He was just talking to me. That's all. He saw the ring and assumed we were engaged."

"Then make sure he stays away from you. If you don't, I will."

"Stop talking like a street brawler," D'Arcy snapped, her hands and feet tingling from the look in his eyes.

All at once he laughed. "You have a way of hitting the nail on the head, my love. At one time I was a street brawler, on the streets of Athens, the year my father let me be a hand on one of his ships. I had to learn to fight or die, so I fought in Hong Kong, Yokahama, Honolulu, San Diego, you name it."

His eyes seemed to glaze over, his lips tightened, his jaw stiffened.

D'Arcy could tell he wasn't seeing her for a moment and that all his memories were not pleasant. "I thought you went to Oxford."

"I did that too. My mother was a fanatic about education." His face softened.

"You were close to her."

"I was close to them both. They loved each other and when I got over the shock of losing them together, I realized that it was best they went together. They were so much a part of one another. I always felt wanted, but I always knew, too, that they loved each other deeply. My father was piloting their plane. He was just taking her up for a short ride because they never flew together, always separately, so that if anything happened to one, the other would be alive to care for me. The engine failed on takeoff. The plane cartwheeled into some trees and burned." Keele looked away from her, his throat working. "Anna was very supportive to me, but I was twenty and had a good knowledge of the business. As soon as I finished my schooling, I started taking over. It was a natural for me. I love it."

D'Arcy stared at that rocklike profile and knew how much of himself he had poured into the business that his father and mother had loved. As though she could see inside him, she sensed the love he had had for his parents. God, she thought in despair, I don't need a reason to love him any more than I do.

He swung his head around like a bull facing an enemy. "We are marrying this month."

"What?" D'Arcy squeaked. "What did you say?"

"You heard me. I'm not having you involve yourself with any other men. When we're married, I'll see to it that you don't."

"You're a crazy Greek!" D'Arcy gasped. "You're insulting me." Her hand itched to belt him in the mouth. "You . . . you talk as though I'm some kind of a wanton."

"Do you know what Greek fire is, D'Arcy?" he asked, his tones silken.

"Yes . . . yes I know what it is. It's some kind of oil mixture the Greeks used, then ignited and threw at the enemy like a missile," she finished, her voice fading at his look.

"It was an incendiary missile all right, but no one knows the exact materials the Byzantine Greeks used. The Greeks are very inventive when it comes to burning their enemies, D'Arcy. If any man comes near you, I'll see to it that he is badly burned." His smile looked hammered onto his face.

"Are you threatening me?" D'Arcy asked, angry and ill at ease all at once.

"However you take the meaning, my love, I think you understand me."

"I won't be intimidated. I went through that once. I won't ever again, not if you kill me," D'Arcy gulped.

With one quick stride, he was beside her, pulling her into his arms. "Perhaps you don't understand me. You will never need to fear me, darling, but I will let no man touch you. I don't think you could ever make my angry enough to want to strike you. I want this lovely body unmarred. Didn't you know that?" His kiss was short and hard. "We'll go out to shop and order your wedding gown," he snapped. "Right now!"

"I have work to do," D'Arcy mumbled, her voice thready.

"It can wait." Keele put her camera on the file cabinet and held her jacket ready for her.

"I can't get married that fast. Henry and Adelaide don't even know you. Sean isn't used to the idea . . ."

"He'll get used to me. Besides, if he's like any normal boy, he'll want brothers and sisters."

"Brothers and sisters," D'Arcy echoed, letting him guide her into the private elevator. She wished the ride would take forever. Perhaps then she would find a way out of the muddle. The ride took mere seconds.

"I want a family," Keele said, leading her toward the gleaming silver Ferrari that was parked in the space marked *Director*. "I'm sure you do as well. We'll live wherever you choose, but I'd like the boy to visit Keros at least once a year. It's healthy there. He'll get to meet and know the family and learn to fish and water-ski and sail. There, he'll learn the business from the ground up as I did."

"The business?" D'Arcy croaked, finding no comfort in the plush gray upholstery as the car crawled through Manhattan. She was hardly aware when Keele stopped the car and parked. She jumped when he reached in her door to hand her out of the car. He led her into a salon with subdued lights and cream and beige decor, soft music coming from invisible speakers around the walls. The ceiling was draped with beige satin much like a sultan's tent. A soignée woman floated up to them, her eyes on Keele. He spoke to her in French.

Before D'Arcy really knew what was happening, she was led into a spacious mirror-lined room. Two women helped her. She was undressed and no one said a word as a turquoise dress with a fitted bodice and a skirt of ruffles to the floor was pulled over her head. D'Arcy was sure it was going to look awful on her. She never wore ruffles. She mumbled this to the silent duo that were sliding the gown down her body. One of them fluffed her hair while the other fluffed the dress, urging her to lift one foot at a time and don the robin's egg blue leather slides. With an exasperated sigh, D'Arcy jerked her head back and up and looked at her image in the mirror. She gulped, lifting her hands to press down on the silk material that clung to her body like a second skin, the tiny ruffles like unopened petals. Her neck looked delicate as it rose from the rounded neckline, her face had a fragile, rosy cast, her hair had taken fire. Her waist had never looked so tiny, her hipline so smooth.

She drifted out to show Keele, knowing she shouldn't be showing him her wedding dress, but unable to resist.

He rose to his feet, his lips parted, his eyes lasering her from head to foot and back again. "You are one beautiful woman. Let's fly to Nevada and marry tonight. Don't even change out of that."

D'Arcy swayed toward him, wanting to please him more than she had ever wanted anything. She saw him move to her, his arms outstretched. Sean. "No." She steadied herself, putting one hand in front of her. "I can't get married that fast."

"It seems that I've heard that before...and today." Keele's voice was low but the words were like bullets.

"My son is important to me. I won't do anything that might hurt him."

He reached out to D'Arcy and turned her slowly, his eyes assessing. "Was his father that important to you too? He must have been quite a man."

"Quite a man." D'Arcy ignored the question, feeling like gelatin in Keele's hands.

"Forget him. Now I'm the man in your life. Take the dress off. We'll buy it. Madame La Rue has a suit I want you to try and she has all the lingerie that you'll need."

"Your favorite colors, of course," D'Arcy snapped, shrugging away from his hold.

"Naturally. You don't have to try much more. She has your measurements."

D'Arcy was dazed when they left the salon. She had tried to argue with Keele about spending so much money, but a look from those gold eyes had quelled her. Now as they approached Fifth Avenue, D'Arcy rounded on him. "I'm not some courtesan that has to be draped like a mannequin. I don't live like that. I could easily have settled for half the things. Don't you ever think of starving people?"

Keele threw back his head and laughed. "A crusader! I'm marrying a bloody crusader."

D'Arcy felt as though she were swelling. She could feel the rage run through her as she clenched her fists. As she opened her mouth, Keele took hold of her fists and kissed them. D'Arcy looked around her, but none of the hurrying New Yorkers took any notice.

"Cool down, angel. I'm not laughing at your altruism. It's just that you are totally different from any of the women I've known."

"I should hope so." She lifted her chin, trying to pull free of his hold.

He wouldn't release her. "You're a delight to me. I'll tell you what I'll do. I'll add up all we've spent today and you can send an equal amount to any charity you choose or any organization. Does that meet with your approval?"

D'Arcy felt a sudden shyness. Before she could question her actions, she stepped close to him, reached up and kissed him, then stepped back at once. "I would like that, very much."

Keele looked like a graven image, the skin pulled so taut that the bones were pushing through. "That's the first time you've ever touched me without me making the first move. I hope it won't be the last, or will I have to give my entire business away to make you come to me?"

"You wouldn't do that." D'Arcy gave a shaky laugh.

"Wouldn't I?" Keele lifted her hand and kissed the palm. "Come along, woman, I can think of a more pleasant spot to make love to you."

"Lunch," D'Arcy gasped. "We'd better eat."

Keele grimaced at her. "You are the most mundane

woman! After we're married, I'm going to teach you to concentrate on me, not on your stomach."

"You think you can do that?" D'Arcy laughed, feeling younger and more carefree than she had in years.

"I guarantee that I will." Keele pulled her hand through his arm, keeping her close to his side as they headed toward the car. "What do you say to dining at a little seafood place I know out on the Island, then stopping to see your Sean?"

"He'll be in school," D'Arcy said in fading accents.

"Not all day," Keele pronounced, accelerating through the crowded streets. "He's only four, isn't he?"

"Yes." D'Arcy's mind numbed, then a small light gleaned. "But he's to go to his friend Jimmy's after school. They're great friends. Jimmy has a rooster."

Keele barked a laugh. "Yes, I can see that a rooster would be a magnet to a boy. I had a hawk when I was a schoolboy in England. My Grandfather Keele had a manor house in the shires. The hawk had been hurt and I found it. My grandfather let me nurse it and keep it. When it was well, it used to soar over my head. One whole summer he was mine. When I was back at school, my grandfather drove down to see me one day to tell me that a gamekeeper had killed the hawk."

D'Arcy could hear the masked pain in his voice and slid closer to him on the seat, putting her hand through his arm.

He gave her a quick downward look, his face like granite. "I've never told anyone that story. I was sure I had forgotten it. You do have a strange effect on me, lady."

There was a long silence. The powerful car ate up the miles as Keele took every opportunity to pass the slower vehicles in front of them.

D'Arcy was still musing over the complex man who was, in fact, the father of her son and would soon become her husband. Would he want to become her husband when he learned about Sean? Would he, instead, try to remove Sean from her life? Would he go away too?

"Come out of your dreamworld, lady," Keele said. "We're here. It doesn't look like much, but the lobster is very good."

D'Arcy had felt Keele's sharp-eyed gaze while she ordered and when they were waiting for the broiled lobsters to be set before them.

"What was making you frown, D'Arcy?" Keele reached toward her, wiping a drop of butter from her chin with his napkin.

When she hedged, Keele's mouth tightened, his eyes an angry glitter. She tried to talk on other subjects, but Keele only muttered his responses, so that lunch was eaten in near-silence.

D'Arcy was glad to return to the car, heaving a big sigh at Keele's stiff-necked attitude.

As they turned onto the highway, a dog ran in front of the car. Only Keele's quick reflexes prevented an accident.

"Sean loves animals," D'Arcy ventured tentatively. "He has a dog and cat. The dog is called Rag and she looks the part. The cat is called Mushroom and is so lazy that she only moves to eat."

"Typical lotus-eating female," Keele chuckled, making D'Arcy sag with relief that he was no longer angry with her.

Then she realized what he had said and rounded on him, ready to defend her sex. Before she could lash out at him he reached an arm around her and fastened her to his side. "Another first. I've never wanted to have a female that close to me when I'm driving. My cars were always important to me. You've changed that too." He frowned for a moment. "I never thought that would happen."

D'Arcy wriggled one hand free and reached up his shirt, running her fingers over him, trying to tickle him. "Don't you dare say that women are lotus eaters."

"You never let anything get by, do you?" He put his mouth to her forehead. "Incidentally, I'm not too ticklish, but you are having an effect on me. In about two minutes I'm pulling over to the side of the road and to hell with the world."

D'Arcy gasped and tried to lever away from him.

"No, I'm not letting you go. Not now, not ever. Just don't touch me with those magic fingers of yours while I'm driving, angel. Comfortable?"

"Yes." And D'Arcy meant it. It felt wonderful to be cuddled to Keele's side. For a moment she could pretend that she really did belong to him. For a moment she could forget that all this would change when he discovered the facts about Sean's birth. She sighed and let her head lean on him. She heard the growl of contentment he gave.

"Where shall we go on our honeymoon?" he muttered into her hair. "I'll take you anywhere you'd like to go, D'Arcy. All I ask is that you consider somewhere private. I don't relish meeting other people when I want to be alone with you."

"It would be nice to be alone," D'Arcy gulped, feeling a shyness that she thought long buried surfacing as his arm tightened.

"Nice is a very mild word for it." He chuckled, following her directions and turning the car with one hand.

"That's the house." D'Arcy pointed, trying to sit straight.

Keele let her sit erect but didn't let her move away from him as he switched off the ignition. "Kiss me," he demanded, his fingers coaxing on her arm.

D'Arcy had to open her mouth to breathe. She felt as though all the avenues of air had shut down. She could almost feel her hatful of inhibitions sailing over the wind-mill. His lips felt cool and familiar as he let her push him back against the seat. The feeling of power grew as she felt his heart thud under her hand. She moved her mouth on his in a deliberate provocation and at once his body responded. The heady feeling increased as the kiss deepened. His hands fastened to her and her mind went blank and drowned in sensation.

"Darling, if we don't get out of this car now, we're going to shock the neighbors," Keele muttered, his voice guttural, a tremor in the hands that ran over her form.

D'Arcy looked at him, bemused and horrifed at the response she couldn't control. Her life was going to be hell when he left her. Her vague reasonings that someday she would find a good man she could live with had all gone up in smoke now that Keele was back in her life. A flash of bitterness, for the empty years she would have, made her wish that he had never come into her life again. Another moment's though and she realized how ridiculous a notion that was. She wouldn't have traded these moments with him even fully aware of the pain ahead for her.

"What are you thinking, little love? Why the crease in that lovely forehead?" Keele whispered, smoothing her clothes and pushing a curl back from her face.

"Oh . . . it's nothing. I hope you like Henry and Adelaide. I don't think I could have raised Sean well without them." She gave him a flutter of a smile, trying to mask the panic rising in her.

Henry opened the door, smiling. "We didn't expect you today, D'Ar . . ." His mouth dropped when he glanced at Keele, then he looked again. "My God."

Keele's smile faded, wariness entering his eyes. Before he could withdraw the hand he had extended, Henry grasped it and pulled him in the door.

D'Arcy could see Keele's puzzlement increasing, but

she felt too frozen to do more than follow the two men. She watched a still bemused Henry turn and face Keele.

"I think we'll be more comfortable in here. I'll just get some coffee."

"You! Get the coffee!" Adelaide laughed, coming into the living room. "That will be the day! Hi, D'Arcy. This must be..." Adelaide's words were swallowed as she stared up at Keele, her mouth agape.

Keele's eyes narrowed, his gaze flicking from one to the other and then to D'Arcy. "I seem to have had a bad effect on you both. Is something bothering you?"

"Not at all," Henry said, his mask in place. "We had a different picture of you entirely. Greek men are not usually so tall and your hair isn't black. It just shows you how false preconceived notions can be."

"That's true." Adelaide rallied, looking at D'Arcy. "Help me with the coffee things will you, dear?"

D'Arcy could feel Keele's eyes X-raying her head as she left the room.

The kitchen had a homey smell of fresh cut vegetables.

"I thought I'd make Irish stew for dinner," Adelaide chatted, filling the percolator. She turned to look at D'Arcy, then looked at the kitchen doorway. She put her fingers to her lips. "We'll talk later," she mouthed to D'Arcy. "Reach down some of that kuchen, will you, dear. I made it yesterday but it's still fresh."

D'Arcy moved like a robot to obey, her hands like puppet hands as she set out silverware. "Sean was supposed to have Show and Tell today. Did you let him take Mushroom?" she asked absently.

"Oh dear, I forgot," Adelaide cried. "Then I had better send Henry down to your house and get Rag. That dog hates to be alone." Adelaide wiped her hands on a towel and frowned at the door. "Wouldn't you think that man would remind me that you had given Sean permission to take the cat to school? Henry forgets everything, even that Rag hates to be alone. It was Henry's day to drive you see, so they must have stopped at the house on the way to school. Why didn't you say anything when you dropped Sean at our house the other day?"

"I forgot."

"Really? I wonder if that runs in a family?" Adelaide looked thoughtful, then shrugged. "No matter." She glanced at D'Arcy, then away. "You know, I've often thought what a good thing it was that you were able to collect on Rudy's G.I. insurance and buy that little cottage down the street from us. It makes it so convenient, don't you think?"

"Convenient." D'Arcy swallowed, wondering what was going on in the living room at the moment. Had Henry told Keele the truth? Had Keele guessed the truth from Henry's conversation? What would Keele do? What could he do? D'Arcy rose to her feet, accepting the tray that Adelaide had pushed into her hands. Then she followed behind the other woman like an automaton.

The coffee hour was a nightmare. D'Arcy had the feeling that she had the lead part in one of those horror movies they kept showing at the theater in the shopping center.

Henry talked about the fishing he had done on the Sound and how Sean was getting very interested in the sport.

Adelaide talked about how large Sean was getting. "At first I couldn't figure where he was getting that rawboned look. Now I understand." She beamed at Keele.

D'Arcy scalded her mouth with hot coffee and started to cough.

"Don't be ridiculous, Adelaide," Henry croaked. "The Kincaids are all big boned. Look at me."

Keele paused in the act of taking a sip of coffee. "Your name is Kincaid? Somehow I thought you were relatives of D'Arcy's, not relatives of her husband's."

"Huh?" Henry floundered, then glassy eyed he watched his wife lean forward to speak, her head shaking, her one finger pointing. Henry coughed once, twice. "You'll want more coffee cake. Adelaide, get some."

"What? Oh, there's enough here. See." She lifted the plate to show Henry.

D'Arcy felt sick.

"Let me show you my fishing equipment." Henry took the cup from Keele's hand and set it on the table.

"Henry! What is the matter with you? Mr. Petrakis is still drinking." Adelaide was aghast. She looked at D'Arcy for support.

D'Arcy lifted a limp hand and watched Henry pull Keele from the room.

"I'll never understand that man," Adelaide fumed.

"He doesn't want you to mention that he is my father's brother."

"Whyever not?" her aunt snapped.

"Keele doesn't know that I wasn't married again after Rudy. He thinks Kincaid is my married name." Her voice was flat.

"Oh dear, this is a tangle," Adelaide moaned. "I don't like things like this. I get mixed up."

"So do I."

"I was going to ask him for dinner," Adelaide wailed.

"Don't. I'll call Sean tonight before he goes to bed. Don't worry." D'Arcy tried to sound soothing. "Tomorrow is Friday. I'll be home for the weekend."

"D'Arcy Kincaid, I have not had a hot flash in years but I feel one coming on now. How can I look that man in the face?" Adelaide folded and refolded the napkins. "God, D'Arcy, Sean is the image of him, isn't he?" she whispered.

"Yes."

"Darling, we were sure that Sean's father was not Rudy, but somehow we thought he had died or something." Adelaide sniffled. "I feel that I've failed you."

D'Arcy rose from her chair at once to embrace her aunt. "Never in a million years have you ever failed me. Without you and Henry, my life would have been so hard. You gave me happiness."

"Oh, D'Arcy, you are our daughter and we love you and Sean so much," Adelaide said. "I will not let that man hurt you."

D'Arcy smiled. "He won't hurt me." I hope he won't, she mused to herself. I intend to keep Sean out of his way.

With Henry's enthusiastic help, she was able to get Keele out the door and into the car. The goodbyes were flurried.

"All right. Explain it to me," Keele demanded, the words fired from his mouth.

"Explain what?" D'Arcy cleared her throat.

"Damn you, D'Arcy, I'm no fool. Those people were horrified at the sight of me. I'm no Adonis, but I don't usually have such a bad effect on people I've just met. What the hell is going on?"

"Ah, Henry and Adelaide never expected me to marry again. I never expected it myself. I'm sure they were just surprised."

The car leaped forward like a live thing.

"I said I'm not a fool." Keele sounded as though he had rocks in his jaws. "Who did they think I was? And why was I hustled out of the house before your son's return?"

D'Arcy's body jerked.

The smile Keele leveled on her had no humor in it. "Yes, I'm fully aware that for some reason known only to you, you do not want me to meet your son."

"You're crazy!" D'Arcy whispered, licking dry lips.

"No, you are, if you're trying to put something over

on me, D'Arcy. Smarter men and women, too, have tried."

"I'm sure of that." Fear made her reckless. "But if you don't mind, spare me a recital of your many forays with women."

The car fired around a curve like a missile.

"D'Arcy, I don't know what you're pulling, but by God I'm going to find out." The car hurtled into the traffic of Manhattan. "And, lady, if you have any idea of getting out of this marriage, forget it."

They were back to square one! D'Arcy fumed, wanting to tell him to slow down but unwilling to break the fulminating silence.

The return trip to Manhattan was accomplished in record time, but still D'Arcy felt as though it took forever. Keele's questioning anger was like a live wire between them.

When the car screeched to the curb in front of her hotel some fifty minutes after leaving Adelaide and Henry, D'Arcy's own temper was simmering. She turned to look at the man next to her who stared through the windshield. "I should think if you find me so untrustworthy you would want to end this engagement fast," she snapped, stepping to the curb and slamming the door behind her.

The car shot back into traffic and disappeared.

By the time D'Arcy reached her rooms, her legs were shaking. She headed straight for the bed, throwing herself face down on the coverlet, kicking off her shoes as she hit the bed.

The ringing of the phone forced her to surface from the well of sleep. "'Lo." She swallowed, trying to moisten her dry throat.

"Were you sleeping?" Keele's voice sliced into her sleepiness.

"Yes."

"You have an hour to get ready. We're meeting some associates of mine for dinner."

"If it's business, you don't need me. I'd rather have a tray in my room and an early night."

"Would you now?" Keele's voice was like raw silk. "If you are not in the lobby at the dot of eight, I'll come for you. And I'll dress you, D'Arcy. Make no mistake about that."

The slamming of the receiver echoed and reechoed in her head. She looked at the phone in her hand. "Mr. Keele Petrakis, I hope you fall down an elevator shaft." D'Arcy replaced the instrument on the cradle with great care.

Their morning shopping had completely left her mind until she opened her closet. Mouth agape, she stared at the purchases they had made that morning, all hanging there as though they had been there for years instead of hours. Who had arranged to have them delivered and hung there? The answer to the question mushroomed in her head almost as she thought of the question. Keele! Damn him! He was taking her over just as though she were a company he had purchased.

She fumed and railed at the absent Greek, taking great pleasure in wringing out her washcloth as though it were his neck. While she showered she tried out every nasty phrase she could dream up, picturing herself saying them to a cringing Keele Petrakis. Fat chance he would ever cringe, a mocking voice whispered deep in her mind.

She wasn't exactly calm as she donned her apricot colored underthings, but she was resigned. She faced the closet again and wondered what to wear. For long minutes, she fingered the blue jeans and sweatshirt that hung there. "They're new," she muttered to herself. "The sweat shirt would be such a nice touch at the dinner."

She giggled at the lovely thought, imagining Keele's open-mouthed chagrin.

She sighed and reached for the soft wool dress in a teale blue, that had the fine texture of silk. It had long sleeves that folded back at the wrist, a tight bodice that delineated her tiny waist, and a flaring skirt that showed her long slim legs to advantage. With it she wore a silk scarf ascotted in the arrow neckline. The scarf was geometric patterns of beige. She pinned a butterfly pin with turquoise wings and sapphire eyes to the scarf. The pin had belonged to her mother and was a favorite. With it she wore dot earrings of sapphire. The pierced earrings had belonged to Adelaide's grandmother. Her shoes and bag were beige suede, the heels medium high.

At five minutes before the hour of eight she stepped into the elevator, hoping that Keele would be late.

To her annoyance, he was propped against a pillar staring at the elevator, his watch hand held in front of him.

"My, my, you're on time." Keele took her arm, the steel fingers forestalling any attempt she might make to free herself.

"What did you expect? Your threat worked."

Keele barked a laugh but didn't deny it. "We're meeting my friends at a dinner club. I think you'll enjoy it."

"Would it matter if I didn't?"

Keele didn't answer her. Instead he led her to the chauffeured limousine that he preferred using at night.

Once in the car Keele turned to her and folded her into his arms. Before she could protest, his mouth had clamped to hers and he was taking her over as though she were a claim he had staked. She tried to struggle but it was as though he would not allow her to even consider resistance. She felt herself pulled into him as though he had absorbed her.

When he released her, his breathing was as heavy as her own. For a moment she thought she saw a strange flicker in the golden depths of his eyes, then it was gone. She was so groggy she might have imagined it, she mused, one hand going to her hair.

Keele didn't release her until they had reached their destination. D'Arcy recognized the name on the club as one which she never had even dared hope to enter.

The maître d' led them to a table off to one side. When D'Arcy looked up she faltered, but Keele's steel hand urged her forward.

"Why didn't you tell me Madame Davos was going to be here? And Elena and Gregor Arfos?" she mumbled.

Keele shrugged, leading her to a chair and beginning to introduce the other people at the table.

D'Arcy knew she would not remember their names.

At once Keele seemed to be drawn into a discussion with the two men across from him.

"It is nice to see you again, Mrs. Kincaid," Madame said through wooden lips.

Keele's head swiveled around, his face granite. D'Arcy had the feeling she smelled brimstone. "Call her D'Arcy, Anna. She is my affianced wife. She will be treated that way."

D'Arcy gasped, pulling at his arm, not wanting him to turn his family against her by his threatening manner.

"What is it you want, my dove? Your kiss? Very well, but then you must let me discuss business." He leaned over her open mouth, hard amusement in his eyes. The kiss was long and intimate. "There. Now let me try to concentrate."

D'Arcy could feel the heat in her face, sure that she would go up in a cinder of embarrassment. She wanted to draw and quarter Keele. "I'm just fine, Madame Davos." D'Arcy's voice was husky, her eyes not quite meeting the other woman's. "I hope you are enjoying your stay in New York."

"Elena and I have shopped." The woman shrugged.

"Neither Anna nor I consider the stores here the equal of Paris." Elena spoke while pushing a brown cheroot into a long holder.

"Then by all means go to Paris," D'Arcy snapped.

The gasps of the two women were masked by Gregor Arfos's shout of laughter.

Keele turned back to look at her, his narrowed eyes taking in the affronted look of his aunt and the two coin-sized red spots on Elena's cheeks. "Now what have you said?"

Gregor spoke before she could open her mouth. "Your lady has the quick answer, Keele Andreas Petrakis. She is like your mother. Ahhh, there was a lady."

Keele nodded to Gregor and gave D'Arcy a hard smile.

D'Arcy looked away from him and leaned toward Gregor. "Tell me about Keele's mother."

He nodded his head, like a bull shagging flies. "She was tall and her hair was like wheat and she could do anything. I was jealous of my friend Andreas, I tell you that." A smile flickered over his face, then he sighed. "She became more beautiful every day and my friend Andreas was at her feet."

"My brother was never at any woman's feet," Anna Davos hissed, her face pale.

"Awww, you were always jealous of her, Anna. Yes, you were, so don't look daggers at me. Andreas shared everything with her. She knew more about his business than he did, I think. She was smart, that one, but always a woman. It is good that they died together. Andreas could not have lived without her." Gregor stared at Anna and gave an assured jerk of his head.

Both Elena and Anna glared at Gregor, but he paid no heed as he told D'Arcy anecdotes about his friend and his friend's wife.

D'Arcy noticed that Keele had stopped talking to his business associate and was listening to Gregor as intently as D'Arcy was.

When dinner was served, all the people at the table with the exception of Elena and Anna were hanging on Gregor's words.

"You will now eat your dinner before it gets cold, Papa," Elena announced.

Gregor shrugged but turned to D'Arcy and winked.

For a few moments silence reigned.

"You are bringing your little boy to the party at my house," Gregor boomed at her, making D'Arcy drop her fork.

Keele signaled for the waiter to bring another.

"It seems you are always causing problems at the table." Elena tittered, bringing a small smile to Anna's face.

"Do not be silly," Gregor thundered. "Anyone can drop a fork. I do it all the time." He turned to look at a white-faced D'Arcy and reached to pat her hand. "You will like the place I have leased on the Island. It is big and on the water. Greeks like water." He roared at his own joke.

"Mr. Arfos..." D'Arcy cleared her throat. "I had not..."

"What D'Arcy means," Keele interjected, "is that we are delighted that you have invited her son, but from now on you must call him my son as well. I have had my lawyer draw up the papers for adoption so that when D'Arcy and I are married, Sean will become my son."

Chapter

6

D'ARCY HAD NO real awareness of the rest of the evening. She made responses when queries were made of her. She had a bemused knowledge of the hard-eyed looks Anna and Elena gave her. She felt a nervous irritation at the amusement in Keele's eyes when he looked at her. Yet there was a cloudlike feeling to the whole night and she was glad when Keele took her to her door and kissed her good night, not once but many times.

"Don't think I'll allow you to be so detached when we're man and wife, my sweet." Keele's voice was chipped glass. "I fully intend that you will have all your concentration on me."

"Sean occupies much of my thoughts," D'Arcy answered woodenly. "Am I supposed to deny my son because I'm to be married?"

"Not at all. Sean and I will share you, but we will be the only men in your life." He pulled back from her to

look down into her face. "And I want the meeting between me and my son to be soon. Do you understand
me, D'Arcy?"

"What?" she squawked, feeling her face sag, then
somehow getting control of herself. "Yes, yes, I understand."

"Good night, my love. Let's hope you'll be more
responsive tomorrow."

"I'm going home tomorrow. I promised I would take
Sean to a friend's party. I won't be able to see you."
D'Arcy tried to keep her voice even.

The pause was long.

"All right, D'Arcy. We don't see each other until
Monday. This is the last time you'll pull that. Clear?"

"Clear." D'Arcy was so relieved she forgot to tell him
that she thought his tone was arrogant.

Alone in her hotel bed, she tried to shut the future
from her mind. No matter which way she approached it,
she could only envision chaos.

When she finally fell asleep, her body and mind ached
and the gray tinge of predawn was coating the New York
skyline. Her last thought was that at all costs she must
protect Sean, that no matter what weapons a powerful
man like Keele Petrakis could call into play, she would
fight him and she would win.

Saturday was warm. Sailboats dotted the Sound as
last-ditch hopefuls tried to hold back the cool autumn
weather. You could swim in a heated pool today, D'Arcy
mused as she steered her battered car away from the
railroad station and headed home.

She arrived at Henry and Adelaide's while Sean was
still breakfasting and Adelaide was trying to argue Mushroom out of sharpening her claws on the drapes.

"Why doesn't she do that at your house, D'Arcy?"
Adelaide moaned, toting the big cat, which looked more
like a fur boa, to the kitchen.

"I don't know." D'Arcy tried to glare at the yawning cat.

"Mommy," Sean roared. "Rag is going to have puppies. Mr. Bidwell said so." Sean smiled at the three open-mouthed adults who looked from him to the snoozing dog under the table.

"Don't be silly," D'Arcy admonished in a reedy voice. "Rag is spayed, isn't she, Henry?"

"So I thought when I bought her from the Fergusons." Henry was staring at the dog as though the scruffy creature had turned into a piranha.

"Didn't anyone check?" Adelaide whispered, rubbing her hands down the front of her apron.

"Mr. Bidwell says that her teats are swelling nicely and she'll have three or four," Sean announced, still panting slightly from his headlong charge through the door, the space in his mouth gaping wide with pleasure.

"Is that so?" Adelaide replied, sinking into a chair. She looked at D'Arcy, reproach in her eyes. "You might have warned us, dear. I'm not sure I know the procedure for this. What do we feed puppies?"

"The mother takes care of that...at first," Henry said, still staring at Rag. "God, D'Arcy, you should have had a dog when you were little. Then we'd know more than we do."

D'Arcy shrugged. "I was perfectly happy with my parakeet."

Adelaide frowned at D'Arcy. "That was always your trouble. You were never ambitious enough, dear. You should have been more forceful, told us you wanted a dog. I'm sure I wouldn't have minded." Her face crumpled just a bit. "But this...a gaggle of puppies."

"Geese," Henry mumbled.

"What?" Adelaide was horrified. "Surely she'll have puppies. I'm sure that I read somewhere that animals..."

"A gaggle of geese, not puppies. I don't know what they call a group of puppies."

"A herd, Uncle Henry?" Sean offered.

"No, dear, that's a herd of elephants and we don't want that. I suppose we should feel grateful that Rag isn't an elephant. I think the zoning here would not..."

"Adelaide, for God's sake," Henry interrupted.

D'Arcy started to laugh, a soft helpless sound that she couldn't control. All at once she knew that she was both laughing and crying and that Henry was leading her from the room and Adelaide was telling Sean that she would pour him some more milk and some for Rag as well.

The door to Henry's study closed behind him and D'Arcy sank into a chair, covering her face with her hands, trying to stop the shuddering of her body.

"D'Arcy, this farce has gone on far too long. I am going to bring it to an end before you have a breakdown." Henry lifted a hand, palm outward, forestalling any remark from her. "Don't bother trying to talk me out of it, D'Arcy. I'm telling Petrakis that Sean is his natural son. All this deceit is taking a terrible toll on you and I won't allow it to go on."

"Henry, please." D'Arcy stumbled over the words, trying to control herself. "I'm going to tell him myself, but at the right moment. He's a powerful man, Henry. If he decides to fight me for Sean, it could mean trouble. I won't risk losing Sean, no matter what I have to do. He's mine," D'Arcy finished, threading her fingers together.

"He damn well won't take Sean from us," Henry roared, walking to D'Arcy and pulling her head against him. "We'll fight him, D'Arcy. I'm not without influence. People in this town know you and know what a good job you've done with Sean. We have ammunition too, D'Arcy. We can fight and we will—if we have to. No one is taking Sean away from us. But do you really think Petrakis would do such a thing?"

D'Arcy turned in her chair and pressed her face into

his vest, her sobbing muffled, the sound of her own crying shocking her. She had not cried since the early days of her marriage to Rudy.

Missy Winslow's party had a clown and D'Arcy and Jimmy's mother, Jen Sturmer, were urged to stay and see the show. For almost four hours, D'Arcy was able to put Keele in a shadowy compartment of her mind, delighting in Sean's delight and the lighthearted chatter of the other women.

On the way home, Sean bounced against the restraints of the seat belt. "I want a clown when I have my birthday and a pony too . . . and balloons and a red drink."

"How would you like a father instead?" D'Arcy asked, her tones light.

"Instead of a clown?" Sean asked warily.

"Oh no, we might have the clown too." D'Arcy smiled, glancing quickly at her son.

"Awright, but if I have to choose, I think I'll have the clown."

"Once we have your father in the house, we'll have him always," D'Arcy said in measured tones.

"You told me this once, Mommy," Sean said in a resigned voice. "I'd like a daddy like Jimmy has, but I want a clown too."

"Clowns are pretty special," D'Arcy agreed.

That evening D'Arcy invited Henry and Adelaide to dinner so that Sean could describe in detail the entire party.

Adelaide agreed that Sean should have a clown at his next party. "I do not believe in one-upmanship, but, perhaps we could have two clowns," she mused.

"Adelaide," D'Arcy and Henry chorused.

"Well, after all . . ." she began.

"S'awright, Auntie Adelaide, one clown is good." Sean patted her cheek with a tacky hand, making Adelaide beam.

The phone rang and D'Arcy was still laughing as she answered it.

"You sound happy." Keele's silky accusation sobered her. "Who is there?"

"Who's calling?" D'Arcy quipped.

"Gambling on the distance between us, my love? Don't." Keele grated into her ear.

"Don't threaten me, macho man!" D'Arcy shouted.

"Calm down, my little firecracker." Real humor edged his voice. "You know damn well that I'm never going to threaten you with physical or mental harm, but I still don't want you in the company of any men but myself."

"Henry and Adelaide are here for dinner so that Sean can tell them all about the party he attended today."

"And didn't you think that I would be interested in the party?" Keele's voice was Antarctica. "Doesn't it stand to reason that I would be interested in my future son's day?"

"Would you like to go to Show and Tell?"

"What? What the hell are you talking about? D'Arcy, if you're trying to play games with me..."

"Sean said that if he had a daddy he would take him as Show and Tell one day." She swallowed. "Would you go?"

"Tell him to name the day," Keele chuckled, nearly knocking D'Arcy out of her shoes. "All you have to do is make sure he gives me enough notice to clear my calendar," Keele continued as D'Arcy was silent.

D'Arcy felt like a fish, gaffed and boated. Surprise had left her breathless. "You don't mean it," she choked.

"Put Sean on the phone."

"No...I mean, that's not necessary..."

"Put him on the phone, D'Arcy." The order was sizzled into her ear.

She turned from the phone like a robot and returned to the dining room. "Would you like to speak to Keele,

Sean? He's the man who is going . . ."

"I know. I know." The little boy scrambled down from his chair, unaware of the strange silence among the adults. "Yes I want to speak to him." His cocky response was so like his father's would be that D'Arcy reeled before following him to the phone. "Yes. Hello to you. Yes. You will?" Sean squealed. "I will. Yes, I will. Are you coming to my house soon?"

D'Arcy's heart sank to her shoes.

"Okay. I'll tell Mommy. Can she come too? She can?" Sean's happy voice grated on D'Arcy's nerves for the first time in her memory.

She started to turn away when Sean called her back and said that his new daddy wanted to speak to her. He skipped back to the dining room, caroling to Adelaide and Henry that his new daddy was coming to his school and that he was going to take him to a picnic. "You are not his daddy yet," D'Arcy muttered into the phone.

Keele's grin was in his voice when he answered. "I will be soon. Don't fight the inevitable, love." His voice became thoughtful. "I feel a rapport with the boy already. No doubt it's the powerful pull of his mommy coming through. I've changed my mind about waiting until Monday to see you. I'll be out tomorrow for dinner. Don't bother cooking. I'll bring it with me."

The connection was broken before D'Arcy could respond. "Damn arrogant bastard," she hissed into the buzzing receiver. Her next thought was to pack her bags and sign up as a mercenary in the army of the Sudan. Then she considered gathering Sean into the car and driving north into the wilds of Canada. She sighed and returned to the dining room to tell Adelaide and Henry that Keele was coming for dinner tomorrow.

The next day Sean was awake with the birds, urging D'Arcy to rise. Since she hadn't fallen asleep much before predawn, her eyes felt as though they were glued to her cheeks. "Mommy, aren't you hungry? I am. Rag and Mushroom are too. I fed them. I spilled some of the food, but I swept it up for you."

"Thanks." D'Arcy's cotton-wool mouth made the word but it was a furry effort. She pushed back her sheets, letting the bed air while she was in her bathroom. Even while she was in there Sean chattered to her, seeming not to take a breath.

By the time she finished making their two beds, he was jumping up and down.

"Does he like soccer, Mommy? Does he? Jimmy's father plays soccer. I like soccer." He followed her down the hall to the kitchen of the small ranch-type house.

"I'll play soccer with you," D'Arcy told him as she whisked eggs and squeezed his juice.

His frown reproached her. "Mommies don't play soccer."

"Why?" D'Arcy asked, watching him clamber into his chair, then tying a napkin round his neck.

"'Cause," he pronounced in solemn tones.

"Gotcha." D'Arcy pressed a kiss to the top of his head as she took her plate to the sink and rinsed it into the disposal. She was reaching for the coffee pot when the front doorbell rang.

"I'll get it," Sean shouted, stumbling out of his chair and running to the door, a barking Rag at his heels.

D'Arcy was irritated with the newsboy anyway for tossing the paper in the wet bushes every morning and now he was collecting at this godforsaken time on a Sunday morning! What if she had gone to early service! She wiped her hands on a towel and turned toward the hallway, her purse in her hand.

"Good morning, D'Arcy." Keele stood there, a giggling Sean on his shoulder.

"We s'prised you, Mommy. Didn't we?" Sean laughed as Keele lowered him to the floor.

"You're heavy, do you know that?" Keele smiled down at him.

"I'm biggest in school," Sean told him proudly. "I'm the troll."

"That so?" Keele hunkered down in front of him. "How would you like to swim in a big swimming pool?"

"If it's outside, I can't. Mommy says it's too cold to swim outside now." Sean's mouth turned down, his jaw jutting forward.

"This pool is heated and if it rains then there's a big top that can be blown over it. How does that sound?" Keele chuckled at the round-eyed boy, his still chubby body beginning to bounce with enthusiasm.

"When?"

"Next weekend." Keele rose to his feet and shot a look at D'Arcy. "Aren't you going to say good morning?" His leonine eyes lasered over her, pulling her apart in millipieces to see what she was thinking.

D'Arcy looked at the floor, wishing that it would open under her feet. "Good morning."

"Good morning." He spat the words back at her in mimicry of her tone.

"I thought you weren't coming until later," she said in a rush. "We're going to church."

Keele shrugged. "I'll go with you. I've been known to go to church."

"No," D'Arcy squawked, making Sean look up from his toast. "This isn't a Greek church," she finished lamely, still not looking at him.

Sean rose from his chair and told his mother he was taking Rag and Mushroom out to the yard.

"Don't get dirty," D'Arcy mumbled, pulling the cord on her robe tighter.

Keele watched the boy go out the door and watched the door swing shut behind him, then he looked at her. Again her eyes dropped to the floor. "What the hell is the matter with you? Are you sick or something? Your face is the color of an eggshell."

"You said you were coming for dinner," D'Arcy shot at him.

"So what's the big difference if I come a little early?"

The big difference is, she screamed in her mind while her eyes scanned the kitchen walls as though searching for an escape route, that I would have had a little more time to prepare myself for this, and not be on the verge of a stroke while you kneel in front of your son.

"D'Arcy? D'Arcy look at me. What the hell is the matter?"

"Don't swear," she tried to rally back. "It's Sunday," she said, her head in the air as she sailed past him. "I'm going to dress now. We have to leave in twenty minutes."

"You're crazy."

D'Arcy could hear him mumbling to himself as he went out the kitchen door. She stripped off her robe as she strode across her bedroom to the bathroom door, strewing things every which way. She turned the cold shower on full, letting it stream over her body until she felt like one large goose bump. Then she shampooed her hair, scouring at her scalp until it tingled.

Keele had not recognized his son; that phrase sang round and round in her head as she put on a blue and green plaid dress. With it she wore a cashmere vest in creamy white that Adelaide had knitted for her. It was the only covering she would need on this sunny, crisp fall day.

She called to Sean to put the cat and dog away and found him watching Keele intensely as the man rolled a soccer ball down his leg, then up and down his arm, and finally scooped it up and headed it neatly. It irritated D'Arcy that he should have to be so adept at soccer. "It's time to go," she snapped, glaring at Keele, who looked at her in hard amusement.

When she would have gone to her battered car, he took her arm and led her to the sleek Ferrari parked in front, the silver paint gleaming like sterling in the sun.

"Wow! Are we going to church in that?" Sean bounced into the car. "Can we drive past the Pesbaterian church, please, maybe Jimmy will see us. He goes to Sunday School there."

"Have we time to do that?" Keele asked D'Arcy, his voice silk.

D'Arcy gave one nod in the affirmative.

"Just point out the way, Sean," Keele told the ecstatic boy.

They did not see Jimmy when they passed the Third Presbyterian Church, but Sean's enthusiasm was not dampened. His chubby fingers almost quivered with excitement when he pointed to Henry and Adelaide walking out of the parking lot toward the front entrance of St. Jude's church.

Keele obediently pressed the button to lower the windows so that Sean could shout to them as the Ferrari turned into the parking lot. Sean was delighted at the open-mouthed response of his aunt and uncle. D'Arcy winced.

"Why do I get the feeling I have two heads whenever I'm in the company of your family?" Keele drawled as he pulled his seat forward so that Sean could jump from the car and run toward the waiting Kincaids.

"I'm sure I don't know what you are talking about," D'Arcy announced, her chin high, her voice as steady as she could make it.

"Oh you know, all right, and so will I in short order," he promised her, a smile on his face, but his eyes hard. He took her arm as they approached the older couple, who were smiling down at an ebullient Sean. The boy stumbled over his words as he tried to describe the car and how well Keele could play soccer.

"And Mommy says that I can't call him Daddy until she marries him, so I call him sir," Sean finished on a whoosh of air from his lungs.

"You can call me Keele until your mommy marries me, if you like." He smiled down at the boy and didn't see the looks that Adelaide and Henry gave to D'Arcy.

The church service seemed longer than usual to D'Arcy. Father Mahon was long-winded at the best of times, having once taught Church History at a boys' prep school. Today's lesson was on the cross and Father Mahon took the opportunity to discourse on the finding of the true cross by St. Helen, the mother of the Emperor Constantine.

When D'Arcy felt Keele pinch her she started.

"Constantine is a saint in my church. We are not so far apart," he hissed into her ear.

After church, when D'Arcy tried to escape fast, it seemed to her that the others were dawdling. She didn't want to talk to anyone. When she saw Keele leading Father Mahon toward her, she was horrified.

"Father Mahon tells me that it is the custom of the church to have what is called the Cana conference before marriage."

D'Arcy grasped at it like a straw, feeling a sense of relief at the reprieve.

"But when I told him that you and I were anxious to make a home for Sean as soon as possible, then he said that we might be able to waive that procedure," Keele continued.

Father Mahon said something to her, she was sure because she saw his mouth moving. She could hear nothing for the roaring in her ears.

She turned, with Keele's hand at her elbow and a plastic smile fixed to her lips, and greeted other people, accepting their congratulations.

When Dina Latimer, a solid friend who had often

picked D'Arcy up for parents meetings at the nursery school, cooed that she should have a bridal shower and some of the other women gushed a yes, D'Arcy glared at her.

"That's very nice of you," Keele interjected, his magnetic power drawing the women, making them smile. "I'm sure D'Arcy shares my thanks to you but I think we'll be very busy in the short time we have before the wedding."

D'Arcy glowered, Adelaide looked glassy eyed, Henry's smile was lopsided.

When they finally were in the car after D'Arcy had wrung a promise from the reluctant Adelaide that they would come at once to her house, she sank against the leather upholstery and gulped air into her lungs.

"Mommy, that was nice. Amy Latimer's mother wants me to come to play at the house. When can I go?" Sean leaned over from the back and pushed at his mother's shoulder with stubby fingers.

"Soon," D'Arcy breathed, wondering if there was an opening in the Foreign Legion for women.

"Tired, love?" Keele said, the steel-edged smile slicing her way.

"Yes." D'Arcy tried to salivate in her desert mouth. "I don't think I'll be good company today. Perhaps you would rather not stay today."

"Mom . . . mee," Sean wailed. "Keele and me is going to play soccer."

"Keele and I." D'Arcy bobbed and weaved mentally trying to figure how she was not going to drown herself. Lord, what a mess she'd made of everything.

"Tha's what I said," Sean said, his lip jutting out.

"I'll tell you what we'll do." Keele threw a quick glance at Sean. "We'll help Mommy get the dinner ready, then we'll play soccer. Then after dinner we'll help her clean up and play again."

"Is that a good time?" Sean was suspicious.

Keele barked a laugh. "We'll make a good time out of it."

D'Arcy could hear the smile in her son's voice as he answered Keele. "Awright."

Dinner was lively, D'Arcy had to admit grudgingly to herself, as Keele went out of his way to woo Adelaide and Henry. Sean was well and truly his by the time they sat down to eat.

"D'Arcy will tell you about the tavernas on Keros."

Keele's smile coaxed, but D'Arcy could see the wariness in his eyes when he studied Adelaide and Henry. "The dancing that the men do is second to none in all of Greece."

D'Arcy shook her head. "I didn't have time to see the dancing at the tavernas but I've heard it's wonderful." She didn't look at Keele.

"And the singing was beautiful," Keele continued, his lips tight.

"Will I see this someday?" Sean asked, his mouth ringed in gravy.

"Of course. We will be living in Greece part of the time," Keele assured the boy. "You will learn the dances, just as I did from the fishermen. Then you'll learn to scuba, to water-ski, to sail. We'll do many things."

Sean smiled, then his lips trembled. "I can't leave Rag and Mushroom. They would die."

"Our home will always be here, too," Keele told him in soft tones. "You will have your animals and your chums."

Sean climbed down from his chair after asking his mother and went to Keele's chair and held up his arms. "You can put me to bed."

Keele roared and lifted the boy high in his arms. "I'll do that."

"He must be washed," D'Arcy announced in faint tones, trying not to watch Adelaide roll her eyes.

The silence at the dining room table was electric.

Henry cleared his throat. "They didn't get a chance to go out and play soccer again."

"Ummm? Yes. Pity." Adelaide's smile slipped off her face. "I think I'll book a room at a mental institution for a month," she mused staring at a spot halfway between D'Arcy and Henry.

"Hush, dear," Henry soothed. He looked at D'Arcy. "Better tell him."

"Yes. I know." D'Arcy rose, looking toward the hall. "The *how* to tell him is what I don't know." She gritted her teeth.

"He can't kill you, dear," Adelaide ventured, then, eyes wide, she looked at her husband. "He can't, can he, Henry?"

"Shouldn't think so." Henry licked his lips.

After Henry and Adelaide went into Sean's room to wish him good night, Keele followed D'Arcy from the bedroom to the kitchen laundry, she carrying Sean's clothes.

"You've been jumpy all day, D'Arcy my love," Keele crooned behind her. "But let's face it, you've been jumpy ever since I first met your family. I don't know why, but I'm going to, lady, I'm going to." He kissed the back of her rocklike neck. "By the way, I meant to tell you that I think I'm going to fully enjoy being Sean's father."

Chapter

7

WHEN KEELE ANNOUNCED that he thought the three-day holiday of Columbus Day was perfect since it coincided with Gregor's invitation to them, D'Arcy was sure she could feel another fissure opening in her composure. She was going to blow apart like a bad watch!

The days she didn't stay in town to work on her notes on Athene Enterprises Ltd., Keele drove out to the Island in the evening. He was like her shadow. They breakfasted together. He took her to lunch. They dined, sometimes on canned soup and crackers, if that happened to be Sean's preference. D'Arcy was awed by Keele's ability to eat the soup with the same enthusiasm he had when he dined on *truite en coleur* and Dom Perignon. The apple cider was in and Sean drank it constantly. So did Keele. When he and Sean watched cartoons on a Saturday morning, they sat on the floor and munched Cortland apples and cheered Wiley Coyote.

Keele calmly informed her that he had told Gregor that the three of them would be staying the weekend. "Sean's pleased because I told him about the pool and about Gregor's gardener, Stavros."

"Stavros?" D'Arcy whispered, her throat closing.

"Stavros has a grandson who is the same age as Sean. Gregor is arranging for the boy to stay at the big house so that Sean will have a playmate. Isn't that nice?" Keele said, a crease of impatience on his forehead at D'Arcy's blank look.

"Nice," she muttered, turning words over in her mind, not finding the right ones to tell Keele that Sean was his son.

Sean called at that moment and Keele went back to watch Wiley Coyote.

Each passing day, Sean was becoming more dependent on Keele.

It had shocked D'Arcy to her socks when Keele rearranged his schedule and went to the Adams Nursery School for Show and Tell. Sean had been ecstatic and had talked of nothing else for two days afterward.

Little by little, Henry and Adelaide were accepting him, so that it was not uncommon for Keele and Henry to arrange to attend a ball game. Adelaide was delighted that he liked her peanut butter cookies as well as Sean did. D'Arcy contemplated hari-kari, that ritual form of suicide the Japanese had perfected.

On the Friday afternoon they were to drive the fifteen miles to Gregor's place on the shore, Sean was so excited that he caromed off the walls and the floor. Henry and Adelaide arrived together to shift Rag and Mushroom to their own house, figuring it to be the easier way. D'Arcy wasn't convinced as she leaned down under the bed trying to coax Mushroom out of her corner.

"Trouble, darling?" Keele's voice preceded the warm hand he placed on her elevated derriere.

D'Arcy felt the heat in her body at the caress of his hand, and didn't try to edge away from him. "She knows she has to go in the car, even worse she hates the carrier, but I have to put her in it, otherwise she won't go in the car." D'Arcy moaned, looking into the yellow cat's eyes under the bed, the swish of the tail telling her that Mushroom didn't feel like cooperating.

Keele lifted her from the floor. "Let me try." He leaned across the bed and reached down, grasping the feline. She wasn't happy, but her lazy disposition kept her from striking. "How would you like to ride in a Ferrari, regal lady?" Keele spoke in low tones. All at once the wide-apart cat's eyes closed slightly and she blinked once, twice. "Good. Let's go."

D'Arcy was left standing in the bedroom, gnashing her teeth. "How dare he seduce my cat!" she growled, stalking down the hallway with her fists clenched, in time to see the Ferrari driving away with a smiling Sean clutching his cat. Henry and Adelaide waved to her as their car followed Keele's, Rag panting in the back seat.

Sean and Keele were back in minutes. D'Arcy had the bags sitting in the front hallway so that all Keele had to do was sling them in the car.

"Mommy, you should have seen Mushroom in the car. She likes Fwawis." Sean beamed from the back.

"How discriminating of her."

"Keele says that Mushroom will like our new house, 'cause we're not going to be far from my school, 'cause I'm going to school with Jimmy. Keele says..."

D'Arcy was beginning to think that Sean couldn't start a sentence any other way by the time they turned into the curving drive. They followed the drive to a huge brick and stone mansion that sat on a gentle slope leading down to the Sound. "It ain't much, but it's home," D'Arcy mumbled to Keele, as she sat and watched the liveried man come to remove the luggage from the trunk.

Keele laughed, lifting her one hand to kiss the ring on her finger. "Did you imagine that Gregor could do anything less than the ostentatious when he was entertaining? He's a Greek who came up the hard way. He enjoys spending his money, but he is a hard worker and he has a good heart."

"I know that," D'Arcy said, feeling contrite, not wishing in any way to denigrate the goodness of the bluff Greek.

"Madame." The liveried man coughed to get her attention. "You and your son have the bungalow on the grounds, so that the young man will be near the stables, madame. His horse's name is Jockey."

"He can't ride," D'Arcy said over the whoops of her son.

"I'll teach him," Keele said. "I have the bungalow next to Mrs. Kincaid, is that correct?"

The man coughed. "Ah . . . it has been changed, sir. The bungalow has been given to a Mr. Hudson who is already in residence. You have a room on the second floor, sir." The man's face didn't change, but Keele's color did.

"I see. Well, then, you take my luggage to Mrs. Kincaid's bungalow. I'll be staying there." Keele's head swiveled to D'Arcy's, the look of violence on his face silencing her protest.

Sean was pulling on her arm, saying that he wanted to see his horse.

D'Arcy felt like an outsider with Sean on one side and Keele on the other. They, boy and man, talked to each other as though she weren't there.

"Bungalow" was a misnomer. What they arrived at was a roomy house with two bedrooms, a small kitchen and dining area, a large lounge with fireplace, and two bathrooms, one off each bedroom. There was a small patio off the sliding glass doors of the dining area, and a wooded path led to the stables, the tennis courts, and the pool area. It was off by itself and very private with just a glimmer of the main house through the trees.

D'Arcy was tight lipped when she thought of Elena Arfos. She was sure in her own mind that it was Elena who had arranged for Keele to stay in the main house. D'Arcy knew that she was coming apart when one part of her wanted to carve Elena's initials in her ample bosom with a saber, and the other part of her wanted Keele as far away as possible. She waited until the luggage had been deposited in the bedrooms and the man had left before turning to Keele and clearing her throat.

"Save your breath, D'Arcy. I'm staying here. I've arranged for a rollaway bed to be brought to your room for Sean. I'll occupy the other room." His lip curled in one corner. "Did you think I'd let you stay down here alone when a man like Philo Hudson was staying nearby? Forget it." He went into his bedroom, leaving a slack-jawed D'Arcy unable to decide if she was relieved or horrified.

There was plenty of room for the rollaway cot and Sean seemed intrigued at the idea of being in the same room with his mother.

D'Arcy had the uneasy feeling that his pleasure was made tenfold by finding that Keele was sharing the bungalow.

"Hurry, Mommy. Keele said we can see the horse." Then he wailed. "But he says we have to wait for you. Hurry."

D'Arcy glared at her son's back as he raced from the room. Traitor! After all she'd done for him!

She marched into the outer room, determined to have it out with Keele, but the sight of him talking on the phone and Sean standing next to him looking up at him, pulled her up short. They had matching shirts on! They were dressed alike! How had Keele found a matching

Black Watch tartan shirt like Sean's? Then she frowned as Keele turned away from the phone. "Where did Sean's shirt come from? Where is the brown shirt that he was wearing?"

"Keele changed my shirt, Mommy. See. I have jeans just like his too. I can use them for riding if I wanna," Sean explained, standing next to his father, looking like his miniature.

The two images blurred before her eyes and she put a shaking hand up to her mouth.

"Sean, that was Gregor on the phone. Stavros's son is coming to fetch you to show you the playground . . ."

"I want to see the horses." Sean scowled.

"Your mother and I will come to get you later. Now go out to the patio and wait for Stavros's son. You'll enjoy the playground."

Keele must have closed the glass doors behind Sean, then come up close to her back. She kept her hand pressed to her eyes as she tried to compose herself.

"I didn't think that you would be so upset because of the outfits. I can change his clothes again without too much trouble." He spoke into her hair, his arms sliding round her waist.

"No. No, don't do that. You don't understand." D'Arcy gulped.

"Then explain it to me," he ordered softly.

"I . . . It seemed so . . . so right somehow." D'Arcy gave him a watery smile, feeling the tremor in her lips.

Keele pushed the hair back from her face, his fingers lingering in the auburn curls. "Did I tell you that your round bottom looks enticing in jeans and that your lovely breasts are popping through your shirt?"

"Keele!" She gave an excited laugh, even though she could feel the color running up her neck as she reacted to the heat in his gaze. There was a throbbing in her, as though she were coming down with something. The pulsations were akin to headache sensations, but with this there was no pain, only anticipation. She was wildly glad that he liked her body!

She looked up at him and remembered London, seeing that same hot look in his eye. She felt cool but aflame.

His eyes studied her, his own a liquid gold. "God, I'm glad we'll be married soon." He stared at her, seeming to draw her into him by the power of his eyes. "I can't wait for us to be married, darling," he muttered, his mouth descending to hers.

D'Arcy lifted herself on tiptoe, wanting to be closer, her arms closing about his waist as his arms imprisoned her.

"Dammit, D'Arcy, I can't wait anymore. I've waited four years too long as it is." He mumbled love words against her neck, his one arm reaching down behind her knees.

"Sean! We can't." D'Arcy's voice had a weak breathy quality, even as her hands threaded through the hair at the nape of his neck, tugging and pulling, remembering.

"Sean is playing. We're going to pick him up. Remember?" Keele said softly and not breaking stride as he pushed open the bedroom door and lowered her to the bed. "I want you, D'Arcy. For God's sake don't deny me."

Silently she reached up and pulled him down to her, lifting her body to help him divest her of her clothes. Her own hands were as busy as his and she could hear him chuckle as she struggled with his belt.

The familiar touch of skull under her hands as she pulled at his hair to bring his mouth to hers made her realize how many dreams she'd had like this, how much she had wanted him, how desperate had been the hunger that she had forced into hiding. Her subconscious mushroomed with the hidden starvation and all thought of denying him died in an eruption of passion that had her dizzy.

Keele muttered her name over and over as he strove

to dampen down his own feeling in order to satisfy hers. His tongue roved her body.

When D'Arcy felt she could take no more, he moved over her, his body shaking as though the feel of her under him was driving him crazy. She rose to meet that wildness with her own primitive force that stunned her with its magnitude.

Any veil of pretense that she used to mask her love for Keele was sundered six ways to the middle as she crested with him in awesome satisfaction.

She would have lain there without moving forever if Keele hadn't lifted her, showered with her, bullied her with kisses into dressing.

When they strolled toward the playground some twenty minutes later, Keele kept her fastened to his side with one hard arm, stopping every few steps to kiss her face, her neck, her lips.

As they stepped into the clearing that contained the outdoor gym where Sean was playing, Keele stopped to let his tongue trail around her lips.

"Why are you doing that to Mommy?" Sean said, looking much like a bulldog with his head thrust forward and his fists at his side.

Keele didn't release D'Arcy even when she squirmed to free herself. "I'm going to marry your mommy and I'm going to be kissing her all the time and holding her," Keele instructed in a low voice.

"Oh." Sean looked at his mother. "Is that awright?"

D'Arcy felt Keele's fingers digging into her side at her hesitation. "Yes, dear. All married people kiss and hold one another."

"Oh." Sean was silent for a moment, looking from one to the other. Then his face cleared. "Can we see the horse now?"

Keele grinned down at him. "Indeed we are going to see the horse now."

Keele held one of her hands threaded through his as they followed signs with arrows indicating the direction of the stables. Sean skipped, singing a cartoon song off key.

After the tree darkened path, the sudden sunlight had a blinding effect. D'Arcy didn't see the other persons clustered around the paddock. Gregor's booming laugh turned D'Arcy's head in his direction just as the Greek ordered a man to bring the horse called Jockey.

"He is a small one, as you ordered, Keele, my friend, and his nature is docile. Go ahead, lift the boy to his back. You'll see," Gregor urged.

D'Arcy heard the gasps of the women with half an ear. Her concentration was on Sean and the mixture of fear and excitement that was on his face.

"My God," Elena Arfos said. "No wonder you wanted to marry this bitch."

Keele looked around, still holding Sean, his questioning gaze on Elena's twisted face. Anna Davos was looking at her with such shocked malevolence that D'Arcy stepped back. When she saw the look switch to her son, D'Arcy knew. She felt the blood drain from her body as she made an instinctive lunge for her son atop the horse.

"D'Arcy! What the hell . . . Back off, darling. I have him. He's all right." Keele looked puzzled.

One of the stable boys came over and offered to mount behind Sean. Keele was about to explain that he was taking the boy.

"Let Sam take him, Keele," Elena shrieked, making the snorting horse sidle.

"No." D'Arcy swallowed. "I want him with me."

Keele looked at D'Arcy's parchment white face, her eyes like burning holes, and handed the reins to the boy. "Take him once around and be careful."

"Yessir."

The boy mounted behind Sean and chucked at the horse who moved out with dainty even steps. D'Arcy didn't take her eyes from Sean.

"Darling, what's wrong? Are you ill?" Keele placed an arm around her stiff body.

"I should think she is ill." Elena gave a high laugh, bringing her father's scowl on her.

"You are being hysterical, Elena. I do not like it. There will be other people here soon. You will not make a scene."

"I am not the one making a scene, Papa. Anna sees it, don't you, Anna?"

The older woman nodded once, clasping her hands in front of her, frowning at Keele's arm around D'Arcy.

"I don't know what the hell is going on here, Gregor, but your daughter is upsetting D'Arcy and I won't have it," Keele said in a hard voice.

"Stop it at once, Elena," Gregor roared, looking from D'Arcy's frozen face to his daughter's enraged one.

"I'll stop it at once all right as soon as that whore is off my property," Elena said.

The forward thrust of Keele's body carried D'Arcy with him. Elena stepped back.

"Tell him," she screeched at the mute D'Arcy. "If you won't, I will."

"No," Anna Davos stated, her voice harder than usual. "Someone will hear."

"Then I'll whisper," Elena said, her voice coming like a snarl from her throat. "Look at her son, Keele, the son she has the audacity to dress like you. Is that why she forced you to marry her, showing you the son that is your image? When did you take her to bed? When she was married to the first husband or the second?" Elena's saliva bubbled at the corner of her mouth.

Keele seemed to turn to stone from his feet to his head. At first his eyes never left Elena's face, then like an automaton he turned to look at the gleeful boy on the back of the horse.

"Elena, you are a fool," her father thundered. "I order you to be silent."

Anna Davos moved toward her nephew, but Gregor stretched his arm out toward her.

"And you, woman, will stay where you are." His voice avalanched from his chest, freezing Madame Davos in her tracks.

D'Arcy felt her body sway in reaction to the force field that was Keele as he stood there, body jutting forward, staring at Sean.

The child's laughter was the only sound until a sentry crow cawed loud and left his perch as though he too sensed the menace.

She felt rather than saw Gregor herd the other two women away, taking dazed note of Elena's protest.

Keele strode to the circling horse and pulled on the check rein. "Give him to me," he told the startled stable boy. "Go!" he ordered. "Leave the horse here. I'll take care of it."

"I don't need anybody behind me," Sean piped, glaring at Keele for removing him from the horse's back.

"No?" Keele looked down at him, his eyes opaque. "Let's see, then, if you can be a horseman." He steadied the horse with a murmur, then lifted Sean back onto the horse called Jockey.

"No." D'Arcy came out of her frozen state. "You mustn't." She ran toward Sean, her arms outstretched, her feet feeling like lead as she strove to reach her son. She came hard against Keele's chest. "I'll ride behind him."

"He says he can do it himself." He pinned her to his side with one arm and handed the reins to Sean with the other. "You are to guide him gently, in the same circle as before. If you go any faster, I will pull you off and you will not ride alone again. Do you understand me?" Keele held the check rein until Sean nodded, then he stepped back one step, carrying D'Arcy with him, shushing her when she moaned.

They watched him together, both of them taut as pulled bow strings.

Sean's tongue was out the side of his mouth as he concentrated, his hands held high as the stable boy must have shown him.

"I did that." The words seemed pulled from Keele.

"What did you do?" D'Arcy breathed, feeling the ache in her ribs from Keele's tight hold.

"Pushed the tongue out the side of my mouth when I zeroed in on something. I almost bit it off once when I was learning to ski." He gave a hard laugh, as though he hadn't wanted to share that with her.

It was hard to get Sean off the horse, but finally Keele just ordered him down and he turned right into his father's arms. Keele signaled to the stable boy. Sean was allowed to give the horse a sugar cube before it was led away to be rubbed down.

Sean bounced, chattered, and whooped all the way back to the bungalow, effectively masking the doomlike silence of his parents.

"He is mine, isn't he?" Keele barked at her as they approached the bungalow.

"No, he's mine." D'Arcy's voice was hoarse.

"I once told you that I couldn't imagine a situation where I would want to strike you. I was wrong."

"Then plan on killing me," she shot back, stopping on the path, her fists clenched. "Because I will not give Sean up to you or anyone."

Keele's teeth bared, his thumbs rubbed over the curved fingers in his hands. He swallowed, his throat working. He took her arm and pushed her ahead of him across the patio and through the sliding glass doors to the dining area.

Sean was sitting at the table. A woman in a ruffled apron tied a bib around his neck and then poured him some milk. Small mounds of crackers and cookies sat on the table.

Keele glared at the woman, then pulled D'Arcy with him into the bedroom. "We have to talk, but we can't do it here. I'm going to make some calls. You can watch *our* son, D'Arcy, but don't make any foolish plans. You won't get away from me this time. There isn't a landlady ready to give a story about you going to Scotland this time." He ground his teeth at her. "By the time I figured it was a red herring, you were gone. The airlines didn't even have a record of your flight."

"I flew under the name of R. Kincaid and wore a black wig. I wanted to get away and hide." D'Arcy pressed her lips together.

"You didn't think we had something, something very special together?"

"I thought you'd think I was a one night stand, that I was easy because I fell into bed with you." She threw the words at him. "I wasn't going to be your mistress."

Keele stared at her, his face a twisted mask. "Get out there with Sean."

She almost ran from the room.

If Sean had asked her in some future time what was said between them while he finished his snack, D'Arcy could never have told him. She couldn't remember a word. She felt a sense of relief when the woman cleared the things and left.

Sean was yawning and D'Arcy was glad to have something to do to keep busy.

She had to steel herself to face Keele after Sean dropped off to sleep.

He was standing in front of the mantel, looking down into the flames. His head lifted like a challenging stallion when she entered the lounge. "Henry and Adelaide will be here in a few hours," he announced in hard tones.

"Why? Why did you call them? It isn't their fault that I didn't tell you about Sean."

"I know that. I cleared it with Gregor. They are staying here in the bungalow with Sean. It would hurt him if we told him he had to leave right away with us, so Adelaide and Henry are going to be Gregor's guests for the next two days while we're gone."

"Gone?" D'Arcy took deep breaths readying herself for battle. "I'm not leaving my son."

"He'll be well taken care of. Not only Henry and Adelaide, but also Gregor will see to it."

"What makes you think that I would go anywhere with you?"

"You will, my dove, or face the court battle of your life. I have the money and the battery of lawyers. I am fully prepared to spend every nickel I have to see that my son becomes mine legally. You can either fly to Nevada with me this evening and marry me, or it's war."

D'Arcy felt every drop of blood in her body sink to her toes. She reeled from the ferocity in his face. "We are to be married tonight?"

"Tomorrow, but we fly there tonight. It is all arranged by now, I'm sure." His smile looked nailed to his face.

He hates me, she thought, trying not to let him see how that knowledge buckled her.

"Do you agree, my dove?"

"Don't call me that," she flung at him, wishing she could grab the napping Sean and flee. There was no place to run. There was no move to make, no hole to hide in, no final card to play. "Yes, I will marry you tomorrow." Her lips seemed to crack on the words.

"Good. Pack your things. There's an airfield not far from here. I've arranged for a helicopter to pick us up. We'll be leaving as soon as Adelaide and Henry arrive."

"I should explain to Sean."

"What should you explain?" he snarled. "That it has

taken you five years to inform his father that he was alive and well and living on Long Island. No, *my dove*, there is nothing you must tell him that Henry and Adelaide can't if they choose. He will be happy as long as someone familiar—is close by and as long as he has his horse. Gregor will see to everything."

He turned on his heel as though he couldn't face her any longer without doing her some harm, D'Arcy thought. The slam of his bedroom door reverberated through the house. D'Arcy waited for the sound of Sean's cry signaling that he had wakened, but it never came.

She wandered out the front door of the bungalow and over to a maple tree already turning the russet and gold color of autumn.

"There you are, little one." Gregor's voice was low but still D'Arcy jumped. "Now, now, there is nothing to fear from me, little lady. Keele Andreas has been storming at you, huh?"

D'Arcy tried to smile when she nodded.

"He is hurt. Like all Greeks when they are hurt, they lash out. Not to worry. I know him. He is like a son to me." Gregor sighed. "At one time I hoped that my Elena would have him, but no, I could see that there had been someone who had torn his heart from him and he could not give it to Elena." Gregor stared at her. "Do you not love this son of mine?"

D'Arcy wanted to tell him to mind his own business but the words stuck. "Yes."

The big head almost quivered. "I knew that. And I also know that you are the one who tore his heart from him. I watched him when you were on Keros...that first time when you interviewed Anna. I saw how his eyes ate you up, just like Andreas used to do with Katherine. He wanted you then. He had made up his mind and not all the scheming of Anna and my daughter would change his mind. I knew that. You think I do not know my son? I tell you that he loves you, D'Arcy Kincaid, and that is why he will marry you. All his anger will not change that." Gregor frowned for a moment. "And I tell you that your son will be my grandson. He is good and strong and Greek."

D'Arcy nodded, afraid to believe but wanting it so much that she trembled, knowing now that she would marry Keele if she had to walk across the Atlantic to do it. Hope was filling her body, her mind, her spirit. "I would be honored if you would be the grandfather of my son and more honored to be your daughter-in-law." She leaned up to kiss the grizzled cheek, chuckling when he blushed. "I didn't think Greeks blushed."

"They don't." He bellowed. "I have high blood pressure." Then he enveloped her in a bear hug.

"What's this?" The velvet voice behind them cloaked steel.

Gregor looked over D'Arcy's shoulder at Keele, his own eyes narrowing on the man he called his son. "So? You don't like that I embrace your woman? You wish to fight me on this?"

"Maybe."

D'Arcy looked at him, anger parting her lips. "Don't be more of an ass than you can help," her voice snapped, the zinging in her veins making her brave. Gregor had said he loved her. Was Keele jealous?

"Don't speak to me like that," Keele roared, his head swinging on his neck like a pendulum.

D'Arcy planted a hand on each hip and started for him. She heard Gregor laugh and Sean call to her at the same time.

"What is it, Mommy?" Sean rubbed his eyes and yawned, standing in the doorway of the bungalow. "Why is Keele yelling at you?"

D'Arcy glared at the glowering Keele and moved toward her son. "He isn't yelling, darling. We were just discussing Adelaide and Henry's arrival here."

Sean beamed and demanded to know when they would be there. Gregor lifted the boy into his arms. "You will be staying here with them so that you can ride Jockey."

"But you will not ride alone. Is that clear?" Keele barked, turning the boy's head toward him.

Sean looked at him for a long moment, his lips pushed out. Then he nodded.

"Your mother and I will be back in a few days to fetch you," Keele told him. "And you can begin calling me Daddy now."

"Are you my daddy now?" Sean asked, interest in his voice.

"Yes." Keele reached for him, his arms holding Sean close. "Yes, I'm your daddy."

"Good." Sean patted his cheek, then looked at Gregor. "Can I see Jockey now?"

Henry and Adelaide arrived in short order and were shown to the bungalow.

D'Arcy was aware of the concerned looks thrown her way but decided to tell them of what had occurred when they were alone.

"D'Arcy and I are flying to Nevada to be married tomorrow." Keele took the decision right out of her hands.

"Good God, he knows." Adelaide sank into a lounge chair, her company smile slipping from her face.

"Yes, I know," Keele grated out. "It explains all the looks of horror I received from you two when we first met."

"Don't blame them," D'Arcy hissed at him. "I never told them who Sean's father was. They assumed that it hadn't been Rudy because of Sean's looks, but they didn't know who it was until the day they met you." She cleared her throat, finding it hard to look at him. "The strangest thing was that you didn't see it yourself. I was sure that you would see that Sean is the image of you."

Keele's black brows rose. "Don't hedge. You know

the boy is like you. His expressions are just like you, his hand movements. I'm not a fool, D'Arcy."

"You are if you don't see that the boy is your miniature," Henry said gruffly. "That's what threw me when I first met you—the fact that you were sure to notice just as Adelaide and I did."

"But you didn't," Adelaide moaned. "And it just got worse and worse. Every place we went I expected people to see what we did. That Sunday at church I was sure I was going to die every time someone spoke to me."

Keele shook his head, looking from one to the other. "I never saw it. I felt something for him but I never saw the resemblance."

"Elena and Anna did," D'Arcy said, then stepped back at the reaction.

"Yes, damn you, they saw something that you should have told me long ago."

"Oh, Henry, he is going to kill her," Adelaide wailed.

Keele pulled back, shaking his head. "I'm not going to do anything but marry the mother of my son and give my son his lawful name, Sean Henry Kincaid Petrakis."

Chapter
8

THE FLIGHT TO Nevada would have been most enjoyable for D'Arcy under normal circumstances. She had never been to the western part of the country and she was able to see a lot because they seemed to fly just ahead of the darkness all the way. But if it hadn't been for the captain announcing cities and landmarks, she would never have known some of the places. Keele was silent. D'Arcy was grateful for the stewardess's queries on "coffee, tea, or..." They were the only spoken words she had until it was time for them to deplane. Keele worked out of his briefcase.

The heat of early evening in Las Vegas was strong but not unpleasant to D'Arcy.

The accommodations at Caesar's Palace Hotel were luxurious, but she didn't comment to Keele, who left her at her door and went to this own suite.

D'Arcy prowled the cream and brown rooms while the maid unpacked her things. She took one look at the sauna and stripped the clothes from her body. Maybe ten minutes of intense heat would take away the coldness that had seeped into her bones. Gregor was wrong. Keele didn't love her. He hated her. It was to be a slow lingering death for her either way. If she didn't marry Keele, her life was ashes; if she did marry him it would be a dull endless pain. She had chosen the pain.

Stepping into the cubicle with just a towel wrapped around her, she reclined on the top bench, one hand covering her eyes, trying to fight the thoughts that were surfacing in her mind. Keele would take Sean away from her if she didn't marry him! But what if he took him away? What if he maneuvered her out of Sean's life anyway?

Her head rolled on the slats, the wood pressing into her skull. She hardly noticed the ache of it. She swiped at the tears that slid from the corners of her eyes. In black amusement, she became aware that since Keele had come back into her life, crying had become almost common. She had not cried since Rudy, then that had all changed again.

She sighed, turning on her side, her face toward the wooden wall.

She came awake to someone shaking her.

"D'Arcy, for God's sake, how long have you been in here? Are you trying to kill yourself?" Keele snarled.

"That would certainly settle your problem, wouldn't it?" She staggered from the cubicle, Keele's arm supporting her.

"Now who's being an ass?" he growled at her, leading her to the shower and stripping the towel from her body. He watched her lean against the shower wall, sliding a bit, as he fumbled with the shower head. Then he gave an irritated mutter and stripped his own clothes from his body. "You can't even stand straight. Dammit, woman, have you no sense?"

"No. If I had I wouldn't be marrying you," she snapped at him, feeling groggy but still aware of the muscular, bronzed body hip-to-hip with her in the enclosed cubicle. "I don't need you to take a shower ...owwww, that's cold. No, I hate cold showers. Turn...turn that off," D'Arcy sputtered at him, putting her hands in front of her in an attempt to shield herself from the needle cold spray.

Keele's laugh was harsh. "That's just what you do need, a very cold shower. Maybe now you'll have an inkling of what I've gone through since I met you. You're like one long cold shower to me, D'Arcy. Turn around."

"Why should I?" D'Arcy tried to glare up at him but was choked by the water. His laugh angered her and she pushed him, touching his stomach. Even over the water, she heard his indrawn breath. Her pleasure was short-lived.

"Want to play do you? All right," Keele said through his teeth, grasping her around the waist and doubling her over.

The pats on her bottom surprised her for a moment, then she squealed in rage. "How dare you, Keele Petrakis?" She wriggled, only managing to bang her head on the wall of the shower. "Ouch. Let me go. If I were a man..."

"If you were a man, my dove, we wouldn't be here." He laughed, and D'Arcy heard the deeper note in it.

She struggled in earnest. She was not going to let him think she was available for him whenever he recovered from a fit of pique. Damn the man! "Don't do that," D'Arcy gasped.

"Do what, my dove?" Keele's breath was ragged as with one hand he stroked from nipple to navel and back again. "I do love your body, D'Arcy.

Then love all of me, she screamed at him in her mind as she slid down his water slick body, before he lifted her out of the shower and wrapped her in a fluffy bath sheet. "The maid is in my room," D'Arcy mumbled, cocooned in his arms, her pulse out of control.

"No," Keele said. "She left before I found you in the sauna. I sent her away." He lowered her onto the silky coverlet. Then slowly he peeled the bath sheet back from her body. "Beautiful, and it's mine," he muttered before reaching down and taking one nipple between his teeth and worrying it to pebble hardness.

"No, it's mine." D'Arcy gasped, holding his head between her hands. The moans that escaped her as his mouth lowered on her body shocked her, but she had no control over them. With a life of their own, her hands began to caress him and it was heady justice that her touches were loosening him from the firm grip he had on himself.

"D'Arcy, for God's sake, don't stop," he mumbled into her neck.

His breath moved hotly over her body, the uneven urgent cadence melting her. One by one, his fingers stroked her breast, as though the tactile sensation was too potent for his entire hand to have. His mouth followed his fingers, the gentle pulling of his lips making the hairs on her body stand straight out. His tongue slipped down her body branding every pore.

D'Arcy felt her body jerk and arch as Keele's love-making entered her blood like a new pulse beat. Her open mouth fastened to his shoulder as he came up her body again. They could not get enough of each other nor close enough. D'Arcy had the feeling that she was back in London with him again. Any thought she might have had of denying him was being burned to death in the heat they were generating from each other.

Their coming together was a crash of force fields. D'Arcy had the sure feeling that she understood what the French meant by *"Le petit mort,"* the little death. She

had died to everything and everyone but Keele and she
knew as sure as sunrise that she would never feel anything
else for that man.

When she would have clung closer to him and nuzzled
him, he rolled free of her body and to his feet.

"We have a reservation for dinner at eight. No doubt
you'll want to rest first. We'll go over to the restaurant
at seven for drinks." Without looking at her, like a nude
Apollo, he strode from the room.

"Damn," D'Arcy mumbled into her pillow, pressing
her lips together. For a moment she relived in her mind
the lovemaking they had just shared. He didn't love her,
but that hadn't made it any less beautiful. "How could
it be so wonderful if he doesn't love me?" She shrugged
into her pillow. "That's all you're going to share with
him, D'Arcy my girl, that and Sean." She wriggled on
the bed, feeling comforted. "But that's only until one of
those gorgeous creatures gets hold of him. Then you'll
be out in the cold again," the inner voice informed her.
D'Arcy raised her head from the pillow, looking at the
scrolled headboard with the radio and light switches clev-
erly affixed to the scrolls. "Then I'll just have to stop
looking into the future," D'Arcy argued with her other
self. "Have you no pride?" the voice persisted. "Yes, I
have pride and maybe I wouldn't do this if it didn't
involve Sean, but there's no use thinking about that. Sean
is involved. Besides I love his father." The voice had the
last word. "Then you're a fool."

She slept until the phone rang in her ear. She spent
wasted moments hunting for the phone until she spied
it sitting on a shelf at the bedboard. "Yes," she cotton-
mouthed into the receiver.

"It's six thirty. Get your rear in gear, little dove."
Keele's velvet harshness grated on her nerves.

"I'll be ready at seven," she said shortly.

The phone rang again before she could roll off the

bed. "Wear some of the new things in the closet. Madame La Rue sent many of your things along," Keele whispered into her ear quickly before hanging up without waiting for her to comment.

She rolled back the wall length closet and gaped at the contents. "You would think I was staying a month," she muttered as she fingered and lifted soft wools, sheer chiffons, sensual silks.

She settled on a figure-hugging silk in shades of green, from deep hunter at the ankle-swishing hem washing to the palest sea green in the bodice. The sari-like garment emphasized her swelling breasts, slim waist and hips, her long legs. Her sandals were hunter green leather and she had a green sequined coin bag hanging over her arm. Her one bare shoulder gleamed a pearl image of her face. She wore the lightest makeup with the faintest blush and strokes of green eyeshadow. Her only jewelry was her engagement ring and the drop emerald earrings Keele had given her just before the plane landed.

"I had intended to give these to you as a wedding present," he had announced curtly. "You may as well have them now." He had then turned back to the papers he had been perusing.

She looked in the mirror at the soignée woman whose red hair swung on her shoulders, and frowned at her. "This is just a facade. The real you is Sean's mother." "And Keele Petrakis's anything," the inner voice said. D'Arcy poked her tongue at the mirror image.

It was ten after seven when she sauntered from her room. Keele wasn't there so she decided to meander toward the restaurant, assuming that he had become tired of waiting for her. She was almost to the lobby of the gaming rooms when a man stopped her.

"Hello. I didn't know you at first, D'Arcy. How are you?"

D'Arcy stared at the smiling man with the receding

hairline for a moment, then her smile started. "Jim? Jim Dern. From Hofstra." D'Arcy put out her hand but the laughing man gathered her in a hug.

"What are you doing here? No, don't answer me until I get both of us a drink."

D'Arcy tried to interrupt and tell Jim that she was waiting for someone but he held up a hand to forestall her, then took her elbow and led her to a table on a narrow dais that ran round the gaming area. He helped her into a chair then gestured to a miniskirted waitress who took their drink order.

Jim couldn't wait to take out his pictures of his children and show her. It took D'Arcy long moments to picture his wife, Annette, in her mind, even when he showed her a picture of the smiling, dark haired woman.

"Yes." D'Arcy nodded, shaking the picture in her hand. "Now I remember her."

She was grateful that Jim was so full of his own family that he never asked her about Rudy, but then Jim had been in her classes, Rudy had not. She had met him at a fraternity party. She shook her head to chase the unpleasant memories away.

"So here you are," Keele said in soft tones, standing next to her chair. "I was looking for you." His inquiring nod toward Jim had a cold hauteur that made D'Arcy uneasy. She felt as though someone had sprayed liquid nitrogen into the air. Frost was everywhere.

"Jim and I went to university together." D'Arcy watched him. "He was showing me pictures of his children. I also went to school with his wife."

"Nice." Keele's voice was neutral as he helped her from her chair and shook Jim Dern's hand.

D'Arcy couldn't help but notice the puzzled look on Jim's face as Keele all but hauled her away. "Would you release me please?" she asked through her teeth. "I feel like cargo."

Keele barked a laugh. "You certainly called that one. You are a baggage all right."

D'Arcy halted and tried to wrestle free of his hold. "I am not going to let you insult me." She could feel the heat of anger coating her skin. She was also aware that people were looking at them in idle curiosity, not really taking their thoughts from the gaming tables.

"Settle down," Keele hissed at her.

"No." D'Arcy glared up at him. "I will not let you insult me because I was being friendly to an old classmate. And I'll tell you this." D'Arcy stepped closer to him, bending her head back to look him full in the eyes. "I'll punch your lights out if you ever make remarks like that about me again."

Keele's etched face looked down at her, then the muscle at the corner of his mouth twitched. He laughed. "Don't ever say that you're not like Sean. You're the image of him at this instant." The tight grip on her arm eased, the fingers soothing the red spot they had made. "I'm sorry I insulted you. I was upset at not finding you."

D'Arcy swallowed. "I was looking for you. I thought maybe you had tired of waiting for me and had gone to the restaurant. I was heading that way when Jim spoke to me."

His arm threaded round her waist, pulling her close to his body. "I would always wait for you, angel. I had forgotten my watch and went back for it."

She felt his lips moving in her hair and relaxed against him. "Stupid misunderstanding."

"Yes." He turned her around to face the room. "Would you like to gamble while we have our drink, or would you like to find a quiet place where we can talk."

I want to be alone with you, of course, D'Arcy's mind yelled at him. "Talking doesn't seem to agree with us. Maybe we had better gamble." For a moment she thought she saw a flicker of disappointment in his eyes, but when he shrugged and agreed, she was sure she had been mistaken.

D'Arcy shook her head at the crowd around the roulette wheel. She felt just as much trepidation when Keele stopped at the dice table and she was about to refuse that too when he pushed dice into her hand and inclined his head to the baize-lined area. D'Arcy lost in two rolls. She frowned. "Let me try something else."

When she played twenty-one, the cards slipped in her moist palms. It made her nervous to look at the expressionless man who dealt her the cards. She sipped at her Perrier and lime and said "hit." She lost at first, then she won a little. When she rose from the table she was about thirty dollars to the good. "I want to buy Sean something with the money," she said in high glee to Keele.

"You can buy him anything you want, D'Arcy. You have plenty of money now."

"Yes, but I want to buy him things with my own money." She could have bitten her tongue as those golden eyes pierced her. "I . . . I meant that . . ."

"I know what you meant. Just remember that you are now a rich woman. You can buy anything that you want and *it is your money.*"

"See what happens when we talk," D'Arcy ventured.

"Then let's eat," Keele said.

D'Arcy decided she would send the thirty dollars to the Salvation Army.

Dinner was butterfly shrimp, poached in wine and covered with herb sauce, and served in cups of braised endive. There was a loaf of crusty bread fresh from the oven and salad of marinated mushrooms and tomatoes. D'Arcy didn't want a rich, sweet dessert and nibbled on fruit that accompanied the cheese board Keele ordered.

The show was bawdy and musical. D'Arcy felt her mouth drop open when Keele explained that the gorgeous singer in the slinky satin dress was a female impersonator.

"I don't believe it. She's . . . *he's* gorgeous."

"I prefer redheads myself." Keele studied the full blown figure of the gyrating singer.

I am turning myself into the nearest psychiatric treatment center, D'Arcy told herself grimly. I'm jealous of the way he is looking at a dressed-up man. Oh yes, it is definitely time for the wagon.

"Do you dislike it?" Keele whispered, a smile lifting the corners of his mouth. "We can leave."

"Oh no, this is fine," D'Arcy squeaked, not looking toward the stage.

She was relieved when the comedian came on, but then his language was so earthy she had to fight the heat of embarrassment in her body from rising into her face. She was glad that was the last act and there was dance music for the patrons. Keele rose at once and pulled back her chair.

"Why do I get the feeling I am marrying a little prude?" he breathed into her hair as he folded her into his arms.

"I am not a prude," she said, stung by the chuckle he gave. "I'm as sophisticated as the next person, but I just don't like smutty humor."

"Or men dressed like women," Keele said.

"It didn't entertain me, if that's what you mean." D'Arcy whirled out from his body as the tempo became beguine.

"That isn't what I mean, but I'll let it ride. I'd rather dance with you than argue."

D'Arcy was not even sure why she felt a sudden pain of rejection. She deliberately blanked her mind and gave herself up to the music.

It wasn't many minutes later that she realized that she and Keele were being watched by some of the other dancers on the floor. She was flooded with pride that the man who moved so sensually, whose every motion fit with hers, was to be her husband. Then she felt a sudden dejection. He was good at everything. He'd tire of her. D'Arcy pulled herself up with a mental jerk. She had never had such a defeatist attitude about anything. Not even when she had been with Rudy had she given up. Don't be a fool, D'Arcy Kincaid, she chided herself. At least go down fighting.

The big smile she gave Keele almost made him lose a step, but he recovered. She felt his hands tighten at her waist and the next time she was swung close to his body he didn't release her again. The quick tempo had their bodies massaging each other. D'Arcy felt her breath quicken and it wasn't altogether from the exertion.

They danced for hours. Instead of becoming tired, D'Arcy seemed to feel lighter, more buoyant. She had never felt more energetic in her life.

"The sun will be up soon, lady, and we are booked to be married at eleven o'clock in the morning. Do you think you'll make it?" Keele swayed with her to a golden oldie love song called "Stardust."

"Let's not go until this song is over," D'Arcy muttered into his neck.

"No." Keele's voice was like a groan. "It's a good thing we're getting married tomorrow, little dove, otherwise you wouldn't be sleeping by yourself tonight."

D'Arcy felt hurt that he wasn't going to sleep with her and angry with herself that she should feel that way. "I'm surprised that you would want to sleep with me at all, the way you feel about me."

"Don't try that old dodge, lady. We'll be sleeping together, so don't try to scheme your way out of it." Keele looked down at her as the last notes of the song died away. "We will have a very normal marriage, D'Arcy."

She turned and walked to their table, waiting for him to take care of the check. Normal marriage my eye, she thought, looking at his bent head as he signed the check. What would you think if you knew that I would have schemed to get into your bed, not out of it. She sighed.

Keele's head jerked up. "Tired? We'll go right away."

The kiss that he gave her at her door was light and quick. D'Arcy had to restrain herself from pulling his head down again for a deeper kiss.

She stripped her clothes from her body, stifling a yawn, thinking that at least her fatigue would keep her from dwelling on Keele.

Her sleep was deep and she only muttered at the persistent buzz of the phone, stuffing her head under the pillow.

She felt herself pulled from under the pillow and the covers by two strong hands around her middle. "Wha . . . What's the matter, Keele? I'm tired. Let me sleep."

"We're being married in an hour. One of the company lawyers and his wife are vacationing out here and I've asked them to stand up with us. It wouldn't look very good if we were late for the ceremony."

D'Arcy shrugged one shoulder, her eyes closed, as she leaned against him. "Doesn't bother me."

"It bothers me." He lifted her into his arms and carried her into the bathroom, using one hand to turn on the shower. The cold water made her yowl, but Keele held her under it until she pleaded with him that she was wide awake.

He stripped the sodden nightie from her body. "I would be glad to soap you down, little dove." His hoarse voice popped D'Arcy's eyes open.

Those leonine eyes lavaed over her. She could feel the nipples on her uptilted breasts harden under that hot look. She didn't want him to know the effect he had on her. She had a horror of him finding out that she loved him. She squirmed in anguish at the thought of how he would laugh at her. She could almost see those saturnine brows lifting in disdain. She pushed at him and closed the cubicle door. "I'll be out in a few minutes." She scoured her head, hoping she could stop herself from thinking of him.

When she returned to the bedroom, Keele was nowhere to be seen, but the turquoise dress with the ruffles was splayed across the bed. Mouth agape, D'Arcy fingered the material. How had he gotten the dress here? Then she remembered what he had said about Madame La Rue sending the clothes.

The dress looked and felt as good as it had the first time she tried it on. She was sure it was too dressy for a Las Vegas morning but she knew that she wanted to be married in it. She picked up the clutch bag just as Keele knocked at the door.

She opened it and stepped back, allowing him entry.

He looked at her for a long quiet moment. "You are very lovely. Here. I've brought you something." Keele handed her a spray of whitish green orchids, then he pinned a shimmer of sapphires and emeralds to her right shoulder. The setting was in movable gold so that her slightest movement set the gems in motion.

"It's beautiful." D'Arcy tried to smile.

"Then give me my reward." Keele swept her into his arm, his other hand coming up to cup her chin. His mouth was bruising, but D'Arcy didn't mind. She welcomed his touch, wanting his closeness with a fever.

He lifted his mouth as though it were the last thing he wanted to do, his thumb brushing across her lids. "Come along, lady, it's time."

The chapel was not the cold, impersonal room that

D'Arcy was dreading but a small churchlike building.

She met the Reardons. Dan Reardon was one of Keele's lawyers, and she met the minister at the same time in a flurry of handshakes and greetings. Christine Reardon was a vivacious brunette.

The ceremony was short but D'Arcy listened to every word, finding it a more moving experience than the elaborate ceremony that she had gone through with Rudy.

When Keele placed the wide gold band on her finger, she trembled. It amazed her when Dan Reardon handed her a matching ring to place on Keele's finger. Her surprise must have shown in her face. The crooked smile Keele gave her took note of it.

They were toasted with champagne by the Reardons at a luncheon Keele had arranged.

"Will you be staying for a while, Keele?" Dan asked, lifting his glass toward D'Arcy.

"No. We have pressing matters back in New York, but I've arranged for us to return for a ski vacation in Colorado in December."

"I'm not much of a skier." D'Arcy looked at him over the rim of her champagne glass.

"You'll learn."

When they were alone back in her suite, she faced him. "Are we flying back this afternoon?"

"No." His gold eyes had a hard sheen to them. "We'll go back tomorrow. I have a fancy to have a flutter myself this evening. Will you mind watching me? Or you can even gamble yourself." He shrugged.

"I'll watch you." She tried to mask her disappointment that he didn't say that he wanted to be alone with her. "Maybe I'll have a little nap, since we're going to have another late night."

"Fine." Keele wheeled away from her toward the door. "I'll see you later."

She was still gulping back tears when the outer door

to his suite crashed shut. She hung the wedding dress with great care, swathing it in the tissue paper before enclosing it in the special garment bag.

She tried to rest, but the moment her eyes closed, thoughts of Keele danced behind her lids.

She tried soaking in a mountain of bubble bath. She felt as though someone had wound her too tight.

She donned her one piece swimsuit with the front opening right to the navel, the back bare to the spine. She looked at herself and shrugged. "I could never have competed in this scrap," she muttered, grabbing at a cap to keep the chlorine from her hair as much as possible. Her swim bag was a constant companion since she swam every day at her club in Manhattan. She removed the swim goggles from her bag and slipped the strap over her wrist. She slung a toweling robe over her suit and a bath sheet over her arm.

The pool was Olympic size and had a lane line up one side for lap swimmers. Despite the crowd of people lining the pool deck soaking up the sun, the pool was empty.

D'Arcy slipped into the water in the marked lane and began her laps. She felt more relaxed after twenty and decided on twenty more. By the time she pushed her goggles back onto her cap, she was panting slightly and feeling far less tense.

She heaved herself up on the side of the pool and walked toward where she had left her robe and towel.

"You swim well." The man was heavyset and looked to be in his late thirties or early forties.

"Thank you." D'Arcy turned away and set her towel and robe on an empty lounger.

"Mind if I join you?" the man persisted.

"I'm sorry, but my husband is joining me in a few moments." D'Arcy spoke in pleasant tones but she didn't smile or otherwise encourage the man. She wanted to be alone.

She dragged the lounger into the semishade and spread the towel on it. She lay down on her stomach, edging the straps off her shoulders. Ahhh, she knew she could sleep.

But when she woke, not sure where she was, she wondered why someone should be dripping water on her back.

She lifted herself, blinking, to look at the heavyset man. "Yes?"

"It's been almost two hours. I don't think your husband is joining you. I thought I would." His leer told her that he knew she didn't have a husband.

"No thanks." D'Arcy turned back to sleep when she felt the hand on her buttocks. She turned around to tear a strip off him with her tongue when over his shoulder she saw Keele coming like a bull at the charge. His head was thrust forward, his lips peeled back over his mouth. His eyes had a death glitter in them. "Mister, if I were you, I would run and now," D'Arcy said in low tones. "If you don't, I suggest you give me the name of your next of kin."

The man's head swung around to follow the direction of her gaze. He snapped erect from the lounger, his mouth opening and closing. He made the dash too late. Keele caught him by the neck and the seat of his trunks and heaved him into the pool, silk shirt and all. When the man surfaced, he paddled to the other side of the pool, got out and scampered away.

Some poolsiders yawned, lifted their glasses, shifted on their loungers, and it was over.

Keele looked down at her, gold flames still leaping in his eyes.

D'Arcy rose to her feet. "You are not going to blame that on me," she began.

"No, I'm going to blame it on Madame La Rue. Where the hell do you get off wearing that skimpy thing. I can see every mark on your skin through that thing. See. There's that little kidney shaped mole under your left breast." His finger stroked the underside of her breast, making D'Arcy gasp. "I'm damned if I'm going to let any cheap lothario ogle my wife."

"I don't think he was cheap. That silk shirt he wore cost a couple of hundred dollars, I'd bet." D'Arcy was relieved that he didn't think she had invited the man's attention.

"He's lucky I didn't drown him." Keele looked around at the sun worshippers. "Would you like to swim again? I can get a suit from the attendant."

D'Arcy nodded, not daring to ask him where he'd been but happy that he was going to spend part of the afternoon with her.

Keele was part dolphin, D'Arcy learned as they swam. She was as breathless from looking at his hard muscled body as from their race down the length of the pool. When she noticed some women slipping into the water and paddling near Keele, she had no hesitation in splashing them, making one scream about her hair.

"What a street urchin you are at times," Keele mumbled into her cheek. His sleek body had surfaced under her own and only his face was out of the water, the rest of him pancaking her. "You deliberately splashed that woman and all she wanted to do was go by."

"Oh really?" D'Arcy smiled at him sweetly while keeping an eye on any of the females that might think they could make a move on her husband. "I'll say I'm sorry when we're leaving."

"Don't bother." Keele laughed. "She would probably run screaming for the security people."

D'Arcy shrugged. "Some people have no sense of fun."

"You swim well," he said as his hand stroked her thigh underwater. "Did you swim in competition?"

"Yes." She choked, her fingers clutching his shoulders. "Did you swim in competition?"

"Yes, little dove," he breathed into her ear, carrying her body through the water atop his. "I swam for Britain when I was young."

"Macho man," D'Arcy muttered, liking the feel of his body against hers.

"Yes." He laughed at her. "I liked impressing the girls."

She splashed him, then tried to spring away. She felt her ankle tugged hard and she went underwater. Before she could kick upward, Keele was there, his mouth fastened to hers as they broke the surface. She sputtered and coughed, aware that some of the languid sun worshippers were eyeing them with curiosity.

"You'll never get away from me, my dove," Keele whispered to her as he lifted her from the water.

That night she was content to watch him gamble, sure that she was in the company of an expert. Keele's face was a mask when he played. He and the dealer seemed to take each other's measure and before too long there were a few people standing to one side, watching the play.

For an eerie moment, D'Arcy felt the tension of a player as she watched Keele. Then she fought the feeling down. You will have to accept that you can't show how in tune you are with him, she argued with herself as she sat at his shoulder. If you're not careful, he will suspect how you feel about him. Yet now and then for the length of time that Keele played, D'Arcy had moments when she could feel his decision, feel his tension just before he made his bets, but she kept fighting it. She feared any emotion that might trigger an open response, that might tell Keele Petrakis that she loved him.

When he rose from the table he turned toward her, not even counting the discs in front of him, pushing some of them back toward the dealer. He leaned down and lifted her from the chair, kissing her lightly on the lips. "If I ever go broke we can open up a casino, little dove. You are a good person to have at one's side while gambling. You didn't speak. You hardly moved. You continue to surprise me, D'Arcy. Shall we have some champagne and dance?"

"Yes, please." D'Arcy faltered at the leaping gold of his eyes as he looked down at her. Her heartbeats kicked into warp speed at the promise in those eyes.

Chapter

9

THE DAYS, WEEKS, and months following her hurried marriage to Keele seemed to make a lie of all the hopes that had built in D'Arcy because of that short time in Nevada.

When they returned, D'Arcy had insisted that she fulfill the obligation that she had to her job. Not all Keele's raging that someone else could do the job swayed her, but she had felt the heat of her husband's anger clear through her. The ensuing coldness between them when D'Arcy finished the article on Athene made all the congratulations of the DAY staff seem like sawdust.

D'Arcy could feel Keele's will straining against hers and though he came to her each night and stayed until morning, the silent contest of wills continued. She could not fault the tenderness of his lovemaking, nor could she deny the heat of her own response, but still there was a barrier there that made her feel helpless.

It was a relief to leave her job and plunge herself into

the interior decorating of the house that Keele had purchased for them on the Island. It wasn't new but the location was ideal, not a long ride from Adelaide and Henry or the nursery school that Sean attended. It was a large house, well laid out, and D'Arcy felt a frisson of delight at turning it into a special place for the three of them.

At Keele's insistence a staff had been hired, consisting of Mrs. Thomas, their housekeeper, Toddy, a gardener, and one helper to keep the spacious grounds and make a special area for the climbing apparatus that appealed to Sean. There was a stable where a well fed Jockey reigned as king. In a separate area of the stable, a fiery chestnut stallion was housed that Keele used when he rode with Sean. He had already warned her that she would be getting a mare to ride so that she could accompany Sean as well. D'Arcy nodded but didn't like the idea of riding.

Her warmest moments with Keele were when Sean was with them because both parents doted on the effervescent boy.

They saw Henry and Adelaide regularly and if she didn't call them to drop by, Keele did. He and Henry had developed a friendly rivalry in sports and often D'Arcy found herself envying Henry when she saw him laughing with Keele.

She had determined that she would go slowly in doing the house so that the old things that belonged to the Petrakis family and the few Kincaid treasures would meld in a luster of true hominess.

She finished Keele's study first, amazed at the number of classics that he owned. By the time she had added her own considerable collection of books, the floor-to-ceiling bookshelves looked well stocked. Here and there she placed some of the crystal and porcelain bric-a-brac that Keele told her had belonged to his mother. The salmon and cream colored oriental rugs, which had also belonged to his family, seemed to deepen the patina of the oak paneling. D'Arcy used the splashes of green and blue in the carpets as accent colors around the room. On the floor-to-ceiling windows and French doors she used swagged-back silk sheers in cream that allowed the full light of the sun into the room, also a full vista of the' Sound.

After Keele's study, she turned to the living room. There she adhered to the Federal look, letting the Adams fireplace be the focal point of the room. The blues and creams of the walls and ceiling were enhanced by the blue silk couch with cream throw pillows. Here again oriental rugs were used, with a large oval Kerman in blue and cream laid in front of the fireplace. It was then that Keele announced that it was time they had a party. "The Christmas season is here and we won't be around between Christmas and New Year's because we'll be in Colorado. So . . ." He shrugged, a muscle jerking at the side of his mouth. His graven face seemed to have taken on a leaner, more taut look since their marriage. Even his body looked more spare, tougher, harder. "If it will be hardship for you, I can get Gerta Olsen to give you some help."

D'Arcy took a deep breath at the shard of pain. "No. I think I can handle it. Adelaide will help me." She swallowed. "Will you give me a list of the people you would like to invite? I suppose you'll want business associates to come."

"Yes, but some personal friends, too. I'm sure your list will include Henry and Adelaide so I won't put them on mine, but you might like to invite those women you were so friendly with at the nursery school . . ." He looked at her for some moments, then turned and left the room. He returned before she could turn away to the material catalogues she was using to find just the right cloth for the chair in Sean's room. "Also, I'll give you the name of the caterer I've always used. Just give him the number of persons and he pretty much does it all."

"I see." D'Arcy felt hurt that he didn't ask her if she would like to coordinate the event herself, even if reason told her that the number of persons they would invite would demand outside help.

Mrs. Thomas was a good housekeeper and a fine cook, but her one outstanding feature in D'Arcy's eyes was her affable outlook on a rambunctious boy, a lazy cat, and a pregnant dog. The only time she had really bucked Sean's wishes was when he tried to bring Jockey into the house. Mrs. Thomas had looked at the horse's head at her back door and had calmly led the horse back to the paddock, explaining to Sean that it was his job to wash the horse's tracks from the patio.

Mrs. Thomas didn't turn a hair about preparing the house for upwards of a hundred guests.

As the day approached for the party, the house began to hum in overdrive. Sean was given his vacation to celebrate the birth of Baby Jesus and he proudly hung his wreath made of colored tissue on the inside of the front door.

He glared at Mrs. Thomas. "Are you going to take my wreath off the door?"

"Not me, young sir." Mrs. Thomas winked at D'Arcy.

"Are you, Mommy?"

"No, I like it there and it is the first decoration we have put up today. Now how would you like to help Uncle Henry and Toddy put up the outside lights? You would? Good. Get your snowsuit."

There were only four days to go until the party when Keele announced that he had to fly to Greece on business. "Anna has hit a snag. Besides, she and the Arfoses may be coming here for the Christmas holidays. Perhaps I could convince them to fly back with me and come to the party."

"I would be happy to see Gregor of course," D'Arcy told him, chin up, seeing the twist to his lips.

"But not Anna or Elena, eh?"

"I admit I don't have the warmest feelings toward Elena, but your aunt is your family and of course always welcome in our home. Are you sure you will be able to make it back in time for the party?"

"Umm?" Keele was stuffing some papers into his briefcase and wasn't looking at her when he answered. "I think so. I'm taking Gerta along with me to facilitate things so I should have no trouble getting back."

D'Arcy pressed the back of her hand against her mouth and swallowed the gasp of pain at his words.

Their goodbyes were stiff and stilted in contrast to the warm hugs and laughs between Keele and Sean.

D'Arcy was glad the flurried last minute details for the party absorbed so much of her time so that she could fall exhausted into the king-sized bed that seemed too big and too empty without that hard body next to her.

The day of the party all was in readiness. Sean was being read a story by Henry and Adelaide while D'Arcy dressed. The black silk she wore had a crisscross bodice that hugged her breasts and tiny diamante straps on the shoulders. It flared from the hip in crystal pleats, the hem just touching her knee. She wore the sapphire and emerald pendant at her breast and the emerald drop earrings. Her engagement ring gleamed in the light of the Christmas tree that rose two stories in the front hall.

D'Arcy looked round the hall and saw that a portion of the holly wreath that draped the chandelier was sagging. She looked at her watch, then again at the sagging holly. Under the kitchen stairway was a long, foldable aluminum ladder. It wasn't heavy and D'Arcy had no trouble positioning it under the chandelier. She opened the ladder on the floor and slipped the stabilizers into place to hold it rigid. Then she eased it upward and spread the legs in its triangle stance. She jiggled the ladder, testing its stability, then kicked off her shoes and began a slow climb toward the offending holly drape.

She reached it, then found that she would have to stand at the very top in order to lift the drape over the edge of the chandelier. In slow motion she stepped to the top then straightened her body. Taking a careful breath she lifted the swag over a segment of crystal. She let her breath go just as a key turned in the front door and it swung open.

"Good God! What the bloody hell are you doing up there?" Keele yelled.

D'Arcy turned and the ladder swayed. She tried to correct and her arms flailed the air. "Keele!" she screeched.

The ladder went the opposite way of D'Arcy's body. She had a moment of horror as she looked up at a crazily swinging chandelier, then she was landing against something hard yet soft. She heard the whoosh of air leaving lungs, then she and Keele were a tangle on the floor, she lying on him.

She lifted her head from his chest and twisted to look at him. He was lying there shaking his head.

"Will you tell me . . . what in hell you think you were doing up there? You could have been killed. Aren't there enough people around this place who could do jobs like that?"

"Thank you for catching me. Are you hurt, Keele?"

"No, but I damn well could be. You're not that tiny you know."

"Ohhh, how like you to say something awful. I said I was sorry. Let me up, you . . . you cad."

"Cad? My God, I haven't heard that word since I read Dickens." He laughed, easing upward but not releasing her. Before she could guess his intentions he had gathered her to him and planted a hard kiss on her mouth. His lips were cold and searching, pulling a response from her own mouth. His arms tightened, swinging her over his bent knees.

"Oh Henry, look at that," Adelaide caroled, leaning over the bannister at the top of the stairs. "Isn't that sweet! Couldn't you find a more comfortable spot, dear? Come now, do get up, your dress will be mussed."

Keele heaved himself to his feet, still holding D'Arcy in his arms. His eyes lavaed over her in the revealing silk. "You look like a Christmas candy. I think I'd like a bite," he murmured before releasing her.

Adelaide and Henry descended the open stairway, looking from the fallen ladder to D'Arcy and Keele.

"Keele, you don't have much time to get dressed. You have to hurry." D'Arcy felt her breath catch in her throat at the look he was giving her, his hands still massaging her arms. Then she remembered Gerta Olsen and walked toward Henry. The flare of heat in Keele's eyes betrayed his anger, but he turned to take the stairs two at a time, after greeting the Kincaids.

"I want to say good night to Sean. Perhaps he'll be glad to see me. Then I'll get dressed." His voice faded, as he did, down the hall.

"I'll put this ladder away. Why was it out here, D'Arcy?"

D'Arcy fixed a smile to her face and lightly sketched what had happened with the holly to Henry.

Before Keele returned to them the doorbell was ringing and Mrs. Thomas ushered in the first of the guests. It was fortunate for D'Arcy, since the first people were Athene employees, that Dan and Chris Reardon were also among the first arrivals and Dan was able to make the introductions.

The caterer had arranged for two liveried waiters who saw to it that the drinks and the canapes were passed. Mrs. Thomas kept a weather eye on both young men.

Gregor Arfos, his daughter, and Anna Davos arrived before Keele came downstairs again. Gregor's bluff good humor seemed to smooth over the awkwardness.

"It would seem that your husband isn't very eager to join his wife after a separation of a few days," Elena observed. "I saw Keele in Greece, of course." She smiled at D'Arcy while accepting champagne from the tray.

"How nice for you." D'Arcy tried to smile at Keele's aunt. "How are you, Madame?"

"As Keele's wife, you may call me Anna as he does."

"Perhaps she doesn't want to call you that," Elena interjected. "She probably doesn't even want us here."

"I would always want Keele's family here." D'Arcy smiled, wanting to upend the champagne on Elena's head.

"But since you are not family, Elena, D'Arcy may ask you to leave." Gregor boomed a laugh, coming to D'Arcy's side and planting a kiss on her cheek. He met the matching glares of Anna and Elena with a broad wink in D'Arcy's direction.

As D'Arcy leaned up to kiss his cheek, she looked past him and saw her old boss at the door, a cigarette-smoking Lena Plantz next to him. She excused herself to the two women but urged Gregor Arfos to accompany her. "Hello Gregson. Lena, how are you. Let me introduce you to Gregor Arfos."

"You have the same name as mine, eh? That is good. Mine is a Slav name but I am Greek." He crushed Gregson's hand in his, then enveloped Lena in a bear hug.

Gregson flexed his hand and smiled at the big man. "Well, I'm pretty sure I'm English, but it's a long way back."

Gregor looked sympathetic. "But that is not too bad. There are some good English, you know. Keele Andreas's mother was English. I was in love with her." He smiled at an open-mouthed Timms, then turned to Lena.

"And you, skinny lady, who smokes too much, tell me about you."

"Well, my mother was a Sephardic Jew, if that helps." She dripped caustic honey at the hulking Greek.

"Ah, is this true?" Gregor took the cigarette from Lena and placed it on a passing champagne tray, then gripped her arm above the elbow, steering the wide-eyed woman like an ice-breaking barge through the gathering throng of people. "That is most interesting. You will tell me all about yourself." His thundering voice streamed out behind him.

"He won't eat her or anything, will he?" Gregson asked D'Arcy out of the side of his mouth.

"I don't think so, but Greeks are unpredictable." D'Arcy laughed.

"Unpredictable he may be, dumb he ain't," Timms said. He glared at the champagne then asked for a scotch, neat. "He has the largest slice of one of the biggest computer outfits in the world. He has a yacht that looks like the Queen Mary."

"That would be just about the right size." D'Arcy nodded, gesturing to Mrs. Thomas, then told her to get Gregson his scotch.

"Well, how does it feel being married to one of the richest men around?" Gregson sniffed the liquor, then took an appreciative swallow.

"I don't give interviews, but I will answer off the cuff." D'Arcy fixed him with an unsmiling stare.

Gregson took a deep breath, then exhaled it slowly. "You win. I'm asking as a friend. Are you happy?"

"I love him." D'Arcy looked up at Gregson, aware he could see the pain in her eyes.

He patted her shoulder. "Any time you need to, come into the office. You can work, talk, do what you like."

"My wife won't be working anywhere but in her home." The steel splintered from Keele's mouth as his arm came around her waist, pulling her back to him. "If she wishes to continue with her writing, she will do so here."

D'Arcy stiffened, trying to edge free of his hold. "I don't think Gregson wants to hear our family squabbles." Even her eyes felt hot, she was so mad at Keele.

His leonine eyes touched every pore in her face before he looked up at Gregson again. "She's quite beautiful when she's angry, isn't she? And she is very angry now." Keele gave an exaggerated sigh. "I suppose I had better prepare myself for fireworks after the guests leave." He leaned down and gave her furious mouth a quick peck, then gravitated toward some people.

"Wow," Gregson said mildly. "He really makes it plain, doesn't he? D'Arce, my love, you have a tiger by the tail."

"A lion, not a tiger," she muttered into her champagne glass. "And don't call me D'Arce."

Someone spoke to Gregson and he turned away.

Before D'Arcy could move to speak to Jimmy's parents, Jan and Cliff Sturmer, Elena was in front of her. "Tell me, who is that woman who is climbing all over my father. I do not like such bold women," Elena hissed, her eyes like onyx.

D'Arcy followed her gaze to see Lena pressed against the wall, a laughing Gregor leaning over her with both hands pressed on either side of the woman's head. "Ah . . . somehow I think your father will survive her clutches." D'Arcy ignored Elena's glare, watching the threesome that had come into the lounge.

Marianne Bolle didn't exactly hang on Philo Hudson's arm, but her silver lamé dress looked in danger of leaving her body if she didn't soon stand more erect.

D'Arcy gave a gulp of relief as Steve Linnett came up on Gerta Olsen's side. At least there would be one friendly face in that group.

"Mrs. Olsen, Mrs. Bolle, welcome to our home. Mr. Hudson. Hello, Steve, how are you?" D'Arcy felt comforted when Steve put his arms around her and kissed her cheek.

Then Keele was at her side and the two women in front of her lit like torches.

D'Arcy looked behind her when the quartet she had hired began to play. She could see them through the open doors to the solarium and hoped that they would be warm enough out there in the glass-enclosed room. She tried to pull free of Keele's arm to go and inquire when his arm tightened.

"Where are you going?" he whispered into her hair.

She tried to fight that snaky feeling of weakness that his look always engendered in her body. "I want to ask the musicians if they will be warm enough in the solarium."

"I would think the sun shields that we installed should keep the room warm, but I'll come with you and ask them. We should have the first dance together anyway."

She reveled in the warm hand at her waist but since it gave her a feeling of breathlessness, she was glad when Keele inquired after the comfort of the musicians.

When he swept her into his arms, she cocked her head at the song they were playing. "Stardust," he mumbled into her hair. "Remember we danced to it in Las Vegas."

"I remember." She lifted both her hands to clasp them round his neck, not wanting to think of anything but being in Keele's arms.

"You look so beautiful tonight, wife. I wanted you to wear what I brought you from Athens tonight but I was delayed in traffic from the airport and you were all dressed." He pulled back from her a fraction. "And then you came flying through the air to greet me. I forgot everything after that."

"I'll look at the gift tonight after out guests have

gone." D'Arcy drowned in liquid gold as he looked down at her. "You should have kept it for Christmas, then you wouldn't have had to buy me anything else."

His hands tightened. "Don't take my fun away from me. Buying for you is one of the things I most enjoy."

"Do you?" D'Arcy was barely breathing, she was sure.

"Yes, my dove, I do." Keele leaned down and brushed her mouth with his. "Let's send them home early."

"Really, Keele, you are such a poor host." Marianne spoke at their side. She looked at D'Arcy and held up her glass. "I am having a difficult time getting a drink. Do you think I could have one?"

"We have waiters for that, Marianne." Keele's voice was hard.

D'Arcy eased back from her husband's warm frame. "That's all right. I'll get it for you, Mrs. Bolle." And then I'll dump it down that deep cleavage, D'Arcy thought with satisfaction.

Her fingernails were digging into her palms as she turned away, not wanting to watch the silver lamé melt against Keele's black silk tuxedo.

Adelaide came up to her, her face alight. "Dear, Sean is awake. I told him a story and he's very good, but he would like you to tuck him in again."

"Of course," D'Arcy said, putting Marianne's glass on a passing tray and forgetting about it. "I'll go right up."

It was a relief to leave the noise of the party and enter the quiet wing of the house where Sean was sleeping. Susan Wiggan, the girl that she had hired to stay in Sean's wing while the party was on, smiled at her and yawned.

"There's nothing wrong, Mrs. Petrakis. I think he was just a little too excited earlier in the evening."

"Thank you, Susan, go back to bed. I'll take care of it."

Sean was lying in his bed, his lashes aflutter, so that D'Arcy knew he was on the rim of sleep. "Mommy, tuck me in."

"All right." She smiled and kissed the little face almost slipping away into sleep.

"Do you mind that I took the chance to look at your son?" D'Arcy jumped and turned to look at Steve Linnett.

"No. Come closer. I'm afraid you won't see too much of him awake. He's about gone." She smiled and crooked a finger, bringing him to her side.

They stood close together, not speaking, watching the little boy's mouth sag in sleep.

"He looks healthy," Steve muttered. "Of course I don't know anything about children but I'd say you have a future football player there."

D'Arcy winced. "Please, I'd rather he didn't pick that sport."

Steve gave her a mock glare. "You are talking to a former quarterback, lady. It's a great sport."

"It's a modern death game for contemporary Centurions and contemporary Roman spectators," D'Arcy hissed back, shushing Steve when he started to laugh.

He put his hand over his mouth and tiptoed in an exaggerated way back to the hall.

D'Arcy laughed. "You look like an actor in an old-time horror movie."

"You are a terrible hostess, insulting me at every turn," Steve mocked her.

They leaned against the wall of the wing that led toward the open balcony over the spacious foyer.

"Are you happy, D'Arcy?"

"Yes." D'Arcy hoped that Steve hadn't noticed the hesitation.

"Keele's a lucky man. I wish I had seen you first."
There was no smile on Steve's face as he leaned toward
her.

D'Arcy knew he was going to kiss her. She knew that
she should stop him, but she didn't.

The kiss was pleasant. D'Arcy had to bite back the
sigh that threatened to escape her as she thought of the
Fourth of July that was Keele's lovemaking. No man
would ever make her feel like that.

She saw the pained look on Steve's face when he
pulled back from her and knew that he was aware of the
same thing.

"As I said, Keele Petrakis is a lucky man." He took
her arm and led her toward the balcony. "We had better
get back to your guests."

As they stepped from the more darkened hall into the
well lit balcony, D'Arcy blinked.

"Hello, Gerta, were you looking for me?" Steve asked
the mannequin-like woman who looked from D'Arcy to
Steve and back again. Steve released D'Arcy's arm and
took the other woman's and drew her to the curving stairs
that led down into the foyer.

The party was a success. No one even made a move
to leave until well after midnight.

D'Arcy was disappointed that Keele didn't ask her to
dance again, but she was sure, after twice around the
floor with Gregor Arfos, that her legs would fall off.

Henry was flushed with wine and elation when he
danced with her. "You and Keele give a beautiful party,
dear. Adelaide and I are very proud of you. We have
always worried about you ever since that disastrous marriage to Rudy, but now that you have found love in the
person of such a good man as Keele Petrakis, we feel
our prayers for you have been answered." He whirled
her around, making her laugh. "By the way, did I tell
you that that husband of yours has just invited Adelaide

and me to stay the night. He says that there is no reason to drive the roads at night when we have a room here."

D'Arcy nodded. "He's right. I'm glad you're staying."

"What is this thing that he wants to speak to Adelaide and me about tomorrow?" Henry asked, his words only slightly slurred.

D'Arcy's forehead creased. She shook her head as she looked up at her uncle. "I don't know."

Henry shrugged, then gave her up to a smiling Steve.

Steve seemed preoccupied as he maneuvered her away from the other dancers. "D'Arcy, it's probably nothing, but Keele has been giving me murderous looks. I don't know if Gerta mentioned something to him about seeing us upstairs, but I thought I should warn you."

Ice cold fingers gripped D'Arcy's stomach but she smiled up at Steve. "Thanks, but it will be fine."

Steve studied her face with a worried look. "All right, if you're sure, but I don't want you to . . ."

"He's my husband, Steve. He wouldn't hurt me." In a flash D'Arcy knew that what she said was the absolute truth. Keele would never hurt her knowingly. He had told her on that long-ago evening in his apartment in London that he wouldn't hurt her, and he had tried very hard to make sure that she wouldn't be hurt. "Ah . . . what did you say, Steve?"

"I said I don't know how you put up with that cold-faced aunt of his and that Elena Arfos. They tell me they are staying the night."

D'Arcy hoped that he hadn't noticed how startled she was by that remark. Why had Keele invited all these people to stay the night? D'Arcy went over and over that thought in her mind and didn't come to any conclusion.

When the guests were departing, D'Arcy took her place next to Keele, saying good night and wishing everyone a Merry Christmas. She put her hand on his arm to call attention to something someone was saying to her and felt him jerk away from her. When she looked up into his gray rock face, she tried to interpret the icy rage she saw there.

He ushered her into the living room when the last guest was gone, still not speaking to her.

Henry and Adelaide were passing around coffee and small shrimp puffs that were left from the party.

Keele took a cup and quaffed the contents before speaking. "D'Arcy and I have decided to spend Christmas on Keros and because it would be a great hardship for Sean to be parted from Henry and Adelaide, I want them to accompany us to Keros for Christmas."

When the flurry of remarks had subsided a little, Anna Davos spoke up, her brows lifting a little. "It will be crowded but we will make do."

"We will not be staying with you, Anna. I have opened up my father's house and have had it prepared for us. There is plenty of room in the villa."

"But you have always stayed with me." Anna bit the words.

"I am a married man. My wife likes to decorate her own homes. Much of the furniture in the house is good, but D'Arcy will want to add her own touches to our places..."

"How many places do we have?" D'Arcy hissed, rigid with outrage that he had decided, without consulting her, where they would be staying for Christmas.

"Six," Keele rasped. "One in Athens, one in London, this one, the one in Keros, one in Scotland, one in the Bahamas."

"Goody." She caught the venom in the look he gave her but she gave it right back to him. How dare he decide her life on a whim! How dare he always be in a temper with her! Well, she wouldn't take it, not from him, not from anyone.

D'Arcy was still fuming as she raced around in the

short time allotted to her before they left for Keros, trying to get everything done.

She was totally unprepared when she went in for her annual checkup and her doctor told her she was pregnant. She sat back in her chair and stared at him. "So that's why I've been so tired...sometimes nauseous in the morning. I thought I was getting the flu. Damn irregular periods."

The doctor laughed and congratulated her, telling her she was well and could do anything she chose within reason.

Chapter

10

CHRISTMAS ON KEROS was warm, languid, mellow. Sean loved it. When he swam in the turquoise waters of the sea he would gasp and cling to his father, laughing but wary. Each day he became closer to Keele and his father never tired of telling him that he was Sean Petrakis now. The first time they took Sean sailing, D'Arcy had to restrain herself to keep from clutching Sean to her. Keele wouldn't allow it.

"Watch him, D'Arcy. He's a natural," Keele whispered, his one arm at her waist as a warning not to interfere.

"He's not even five years old," she said through dry lips.

"And you don't trust me to keep my son from harm, is that it?" He ground out the words into her ear, his eyes never leaving the boy who sat on the other side of the tiller from him. "You made a mistake not trusting me the first time we met, D'Arcy. Why do you keep compounding the mistake?"

"I do trust you with Sean," she said, the words struggling from a parched throat as she watched her husband's golden body, clad only in the briefest silk, the dark arrow of hair on his chest pointing into the briefs. He was a beautiful man and she loved him beyond reason. She had felt every hair on that body against her own naked form, for despite their differences, Keele came to her each night and held her until dawn. It was getting more difficult to hold back the cries of love that rose in her throat each night, but each morning she was more determined than ever that Keele not know how she felt about him.

Tennis was another game that Keele introduced his son to and this while he played D'Arcy to love in three games. She glared at the hard amusement in his eyes when she failed to return a forehand drive that just hit the base line. As usual, Sean loved trying; more often than not his tongue protruded from his mouth as he listened to his father and then tried to emulate him.

Christmas Day dawned bright and shining and Sean was delighted with his toys—a truck carrying miniature logs and a fishing rod. Neither D'Arcy nor Keele wanted him spoiled with too many gifts. Later in the day a call came from the States to tell Sean that Rag had given birth to four puppies and that mother and babies were doing well. Sean considered that another Christmas gift and couldn't wait to tell Henry and Adelaide. Since Gregor and Elena would be accompanying Anna Davos to the house for a Christmas dinner, Sean made everyone promise that they would let him make the announcement about Rag.

Gregor as usual overdid it. He brought Sean a pony that he could ride on Keros, with a red saddle, intricately carved.

"I told him that it was wrong," Anna said through pursed lips. "He will spoil the boy."

"I told him that as well." Elena looked at her father with a curled lip.

"Be quiet, the two of you," Gregor roared, watching Keele lead Sean around the white stone drive. "He will not be spoiled. He has good stuff in him."

Henry patted Gregor on the arm. The two men had become good friends and often had an amicable war on the chessboard. "I agree with you, my friend. He has good stuff in him."

"Yes, but he should not be indulged with too many material things. Nothing truly belongs to you until you give it away. That is the way that D'Arcy was raised," Adelaide responded, her usually soft mouth firm and resolute.

"He would be a fool if he gave away Petrakis money," Anna said stiffly.

"Indeed he would," Elena agreed.

D'Arcy could feel herself swell in defense of her aunt. Before she could say anything, Gregor thundered at the two women.

"What would you know of anything? I will give him my money to give away if he wants it." The bearlike Greek thrust his chin forward as though daring the two women to answer him.

When Sean was finally coaxed from the pony, they sat down to dinner. Keele had insisted that they have a traditional dinner of turkey and cranberry sauce because his son had told him how much he liked that.

"Sean will be staying here for several more days with Henry and Adelaide." His bland tone brought D'Arcy's head up. "My wife and I will be heading to Colorado for a ski vacation that I arranged while we were in Nevada getting married."

When D'Arcy was about to protest that she didn't want to leave Sean, Henry rose to his feet, his glance sliding away from D'Arcy's.

"I propose a toast. To my nephew-in-law who is providing a much needed vacation in the sun for my wife and me and it won't do Sean a bit of harm either." Henry raised his glass, the others did the same.

D'Arcy glared at her uncle. He had euchred her, knowing full well that she couldn't protest about wanting to stay with Sean after remarks like that. He was a traitor, D'Arcy thought, grinding her teeth.

It seemed to her that Henry and Adelaide conspired with Keele to get her packed and loaded on the helicopter for the flight to Athens.

Then Keele took over, not allowing her to speak almost until she was on the plane winging back to the States. She was groggy by the time she had boarded another jet for the flight to Colorado and the lovely ski resort of Aspen.

The chalet that Keele had leased for them clung halfway up a mountain like a jewel in the snow.

D'Arcy had a feeling of being the only person on the planet as she stood staring out the window wall of the chalet at the dots on the snow that were people skiing down the mountain.

"You'll like it, D'Arcy. I've already arranged for lessons for you in the morning, and in the afternoons I'll be taking you out myself."

She expelled a deep breath. "Why do I have the feeling that I could come cartwheeling down that slope and end up draped in liniment and bandages?" She allowed herself to lean back on her husband's muscular chest. She could feel the rumble of his laughter at her back.

"No way. I wouldn't let it happen."

For some strange reason D'Arcy relaxed, believing that if Keele said it wouldn't happen, it wouldn't.

They decided to have dinner at a Rathskeller Keele knew that specialized in German dishes.

Keele woke her from her nap to tell her this.

"Don't tell me, let me guess. You used to ski here. Right?" D'Arcy looked up at him leaning over her, one hand on either side of her body.

"Right." Keele laughed. "I studied for a year at UCLA and whenever we could we used to fly into Aspen and ski."

"Rough life you've had, mister." D'Arcy tried not to let him see how affected she was by his nearness. It always made her nervous when Keele became amorous in the daylight. She felt more protected in the dark where he couldn't read the love in her eyes.

"The toughest part of my life has been dealing with you, lady, convincing you that your place is with me," Keele rumbled, his eyes on her mouth, those leonine eyes narrowing when she licked her dry lips. "I have the feeling that I'll never really tame you."

"You won't," D'Arcy said firmly yet through shaking lips. She tried to hold his gaze as his mouth came toward her but her lashes fell on her cheeks.

His mouth grazed hers, a rough gentleness that sent her pulse into high gear. His lips chased over her cheeks and to each ear, then down her neck.

D'Arcy could feel her body arching toward his as his mouth teased her. "Stop it. I should get dressed for dinner."

"I was just thinking of unwrapping that sheet from you," Keele mumbled into her neck, his nose nuzzling the sheet further from her body.

"We'll be late."

"For what?" His hand brushed across her breasts, bringing the sheet away. "Ummm, you taste so good. I won't need a dinner after all..."

"Ohhhh, Keele, don't..." D'Arcy groaned, feeling his mouth travel down her body, her navel contracting with sensation.

"Relax, little dove, relax." Keele's mouth and hands made featherlike forays into the valleys and caves of her body, igniting a fire that seemed to pour from every vein.

She could feel her breath coming in short pants as though she were losing her lung power. *"Agapi mou,* you are mine."

"Yes," D'Arcy sobbed, her arms wrapping around him, her form molding to his.

They crested together with a gush of feeling that seemed mint new to D'Arcy.

"Tell me that no other man has ever made you feel this way, my own. Tell me." Keele still clutched her to him, his face still pressed to her body.

"No other man has ever made me feel this way," D'Arcy said, hating him to know that, afraid that she would lose him if he knew how much she loved him.

He lifted his head and stared down at her for long moments, unsmiling, then he rolled free of her, out of the bed and to his feet. He stretched, his Adonis body gleaming like a statue in the rays of dying sun pouring through the window. He turned to look down at her. "Come and shower with me."

"I...I have to shampoo my hair," D'Arcy stuttered, not able to stop looking at him.

"Fine." He shrugged, reaching down a hand to her. "I'll do it for you. Then you can do mine." The hot, liquid look in those lion's eyes gave her the feeling that her heart was fibrillating.

The shower was fun and Keele seemed determined to make it so. He teased her, washed her, caressed her, until D'Arcy was sure that they were going to forego food altogether.

Keele rinsed them both, then lifted her into a fluffy bath sheet. "D'Arcy, you had better dry yourself. I have the feeling that if I did it, we would go back to bed."

She laughed, feeling young and carefree. She was with Keele. She had him to herself for six days. Perhaps in that time she could make him love her a little. Oh, she knew that she had a strong hold on him through

Sean—and through sex—but she wanted more. She wanted him to want her just because she was D'Arcy, not because she was Sean's mother.

Keele had told her to dress casually, that ski pants and après-ski boots would be fine for the place he was taking her.

She had no idea how he managed to get the snowmobile, but she didn't bother to ask him, knowing by now that when Keele Petrakis wanted something, he reached for it and it was there.

Her face was protected by the plexiglass visor on the helmet she wore, but still when they entered the door to descend to the Rathskeller she could feel that the cold had reddened her cheeks.

The round tables were oak, small but sturdy. Keele again surprised her by ordering their dinner in German, then going to the bar and bringing back two foaming steins of beer.

"Are you sure we're in America?" D'Arcy wiped foam from her lip and looked at Keele.

"Wait, you missed some." He leaned over and placed his mouth over hers, sucking gently on her lower lip. "God, woman." He leaned back in his chair. "You have a power over me." His eyes never left hers as he lifted his stein in a salute to her.

She lifted hers and touched it lightly to his. "I like the beer and that's funny because I don't usually drink the stuff."

"You don't usually drink anything alcoholic," Keele chided her. "I don't know why, but I like that. I have never in my life been bothered by what women do, how they dress, anything..." He lifted a shoulder, as though he found his shirt too tight. "With you, it's different. I want to know everything you do. It knocks the hell out of me that you have such good taste. I love your clothes, the way you do the house. I can't ever remember thinking about it before, let alone caring." He tipped the stein into his mouth, then set it down and looked around the small smoky room.

D'Arcy felt dry-mouthed. She couldn't have said anything if a cattle prod had been put to her. She reeled with the thought that he must care to speak that way. She scolded herself for being too quick. It was the German beer. It made him talk funny.

The food was very hot and very good. Keele laughed when her spaetzle kept dropping from her fork. She almost burned her mouth on the sauerbraten. Twice Keele wiped gravy from her chin. Finally he hitched his chair closer to hers.

"I'm going to arrange to have you strapped in the youth chair the next time we come." He laughed at her when she groped for her beer and took a deep swallow to cool her stinging mouth.

D'Arcy glared at him, fanning her mouth. "What a monster you are, laughing at me when I'm burning to death." She held up her stein. "I need more beer."

Keele laughed and shook his head. "I'll have to lash you to me for the trip home if you have much more." He rose and went to the little bar, returning with two filled steins.

D'Arcy wanted to have some of the cheese kuchen, but she couldn't find the room.

The dancing was energetic and welcome after such a heavy meal. In between dances, the musicians would raise their steins and sing a song called *"Ein Prosit,"* then they would salute each other and drink.

D'Arcy was having a wonderful time. It amazed her how good the beer tasted after the lively ethnic dances. She clung to Keele and laughed and jumped eagerly to her feet when each dance began. It delighted her that her husband knew all the steps and never seemed to tire of dancing with her.

Once they returned to their table, instead of sitting in her own seat, D'Arcy plopped herself into Keele's lap and lifted his stein to her mouth.

"No one in this room would guess that I had a career photographer in my lap. And no one here would guess that you're old enough to be a mother." He nuzzled her ear, holding her close to him, but taking the stein from her grasp. "Enough of that, I think. I don't want you getting sick."

D'Arcy felt lazy, yet on fire and reckless. She let her lips run down his cheek. "Would you be sad if I was sick?" D'Arcy babbled into his face.

"Yes," Keele said, not turning his head, an amused look on his face.

Under the hand she had pressed to his chest, D'Arcy felt his heart accelerate. He wasn't as indifferent as his smile seemed to indicate.

"Then you'll just have to take good care of me." D'Arcy nibbled at his earlobe.

Keele surged to his feet, letting her slide down his body but not releasing her. "I'll pay the bill."

D'Arcy felt his hands linger on her shoulders as he helped her into her down jacket. He zipped her up tight, tying her hood under her chin.

Outside the wind was down, but the night was crystal clear and crisply cold. The stars looked like ice chips on black velvet, the moon like a pearl. She clung to Keele on the trip back, eyes closed, wishing on the moon that she could be close to him always.

He lifted her off the snowmobile and carried her into the house, shutting the door with his foot. He didn't even pause in the lower area but strode straight up the stairs and to the bedroom.

He lowered her onto the bed. When he would have lifted up, D'Arcy tightened her hands on his neck, pulling him down to her. Their clothes were dispatched with a speed that was remarkable if they had thought about it. Their thoughts, hands, and mouths concentrated only on each other. They made love in total silence, then fell asleep in each other's arms.

In the morning she woke first, feeling happy, not wanting to move, knowing that she would be sick when she did. She raised her head and felt the first queasiness. She made it to the bathroom in time for the wrenching nausea to spend itself. She felt a cool hand on her head as she gasped for air.

"I had a feeling that was too much beer for you. You're not used to it." Keele lifted her to her feet, then took a warm, moist cloth to her face. His expression showed concern for her. "You should stay in bed this morning. I'll cancel the ski lesson."

"No need to do that," D'Arcy said, leaning against him while he wiped her face. "It wasn't the beer. I danced most of that away." She looked up at him and grinned. "You're going to be a father again."

"What? Are you sure? Are you well?" He swept her up into his arms. "That damned long plane ride couldn't have been good for you." He strode from the bathroom into their room, holding her against his naked body.

She lay back against the pillows, watching him as he climbed in beside her and gathered her to him. "It tired me, but I'm fine really. My doctor said anything within reason and he said it would be fine as long as I didn't overdo. You go along and ski and I'll take my lesson."

"No," Keele growled into her forehead. "Where you go, that's where I'll be. Are you warm?"

"Umm, toasty." D'Arcy never wanted to move away from him.

After a warm shower, she and Keele dressed, smiling at each other. He seemed to be wherever she was. He insisted on fitting her walking boots to her feet, then on putting extra sweaters and socks into his pack for her.

They breakfasted in the main lodge on eggs and ham. Then Keele introduced her to her instructor and told the handsome young man that he would be coming along.

Keele fussed so much about putting on her skis and making sure it wasn't too windy that D'Arcy was embarrassed.

She found the lesson on the beginner's hill more fun after she was able to dissuade Keele from staying with her and assuring him that she would be more comfortable if he did his runs while she had her lessons. She was aghast at the amount of instruction he heaped on the head of Carl, the teacher, before he would finally leave.

"Whew." Carl pretended to wipe his forehead. "I've heard about guys like that, but I didn't think they could be this bad. He's crazy about you, isn't he?" Carl grinned as he showed her the stem christie.

"Is he?" D'Arcy looked at him hopefully.

"You're quite a kidder, Mrs. Petrakis."

Carl assured D'Arcy that she would be on the intermediate hill before the end of the week as he watched her snowplow to a stop. Then he shook her hand and said he would see her tomorrow.

D'Arcy nodded, then went to the lift.

"Where do you think you're going?"

"Keele! I thought you went up the mountain." D'Arcy rocked on her skis as she watched him move in effortless grace toward her.

"I did and skied down." He reached her and squinted into her face. "Are you sure you're not cold?"

"No. I had a hot chocolate with Carl. I would like to try to ski some more."

"All right, but I won't let you get tired," Keele warned her.

The skiing down was exhilarating. D'Arcy found it easier than getting off the lift. When she stumbled doing that, Keele was there to hold her.

That night they dressed for dinner. Keele hired a car to take them the short distance to the restaurant.

They had lemon sole and crepes.

"Your appetite is so good at any time that I wouldn't be able to guess that you're pregnant." He frowned at her through the smoke of the Corona Colorado he was rolling between his fingers. "Which makes the episode with the ladder far more serious, D'Arcy. You could have aborted if I hadn't been there to catch you."

"Yes, I know, but in my defense I didn't guess then that I was pregnant. It wasn't until I went to Dr. Steeler for my physical that he discovered it. I'm always so irregular, I didn't think anything of it when I missed a period." She reddened under his gaze, glad when he took her hand to lead her to the dance floor.

"I always loved dancing, but with you I'm addicted to it." His breath feathered her cheek. "I had the feeling that my wife was trying to seduce me last night," he drawled after long moments of turning round the floor in silence.

D'Arcy pulled back from him, irrationally angry that he should be so perceptive. "Would that anger you?"

"God, D'Arcy, the thought of it made me so happy, I couldn't get up the stairs fast enough last night." His lips gnawed at her ear as he leaned over her. "After Rudy's funeral I tried so hard to find you," Keele breathed, their tightly locked bodies merely swaying to the music. "The detectives I had looking for you weren't able to trace you in the States at first. They were back-tracking at the university Alessio attended when you turned up on Keros. That's the closest I've ever come to passing out, when I turned and saw you in Anna's lounge."

"Me too." D'Arcy stroked the crisp hair at his nape. She had the strangest feeling as she looked up into his face and saw the gold fire of his eyes as they touched every pore of her face. He had looked at her like that in London and had both frightened and titillated her.

"Did you ever think of our night together?" Keele's face looked hewn from rock, the bones pushing through the too taut skin.

D'Arcy swallowed, wanting to look away from those gold laser eyes, wanting to tell him "no." She had the feeling that if she looked over her shoulder she would see her bastions crumbling, her bridges burning, her defenses flattened. "Yes." Her voice was hoarse and she couldn't seem to clear it. "There were some days that I only thought of you a little, but I had to be working at top speed."

Keele's throat worked as though he had swallowed a stone. His lips parted, but no words came, as both arms enveloped her, his fingers kneading her skin.

D'Arcy looked back at him, awed by the unpeeled look in his face. Hope sprang up like a fountain in her. "When I was far along with Sean, I used to put my hand there and feel him leaping and was so sure he would be a boy, just like you, and I was glad."

"D'Arcy," Keele groaned, his eyes glazed as he looked around him. "We have to go home."

On the short ride home, his one arm kept her close to his side, his chin rubbing her hair. He insisted on lifting her from the car, cradling her like a baby in his arms. "I'm caring for you now."

He lowered her onto the large couch in the living room, then put a taper to the newly built fire. He sat down next to her, pulling her into his arms. "Was it bad for you, D'Arcy? Having Sean, I mean?"

She looked up at him, savoring the emotion she saw there, the open want. "Well, the first one is usually the worst, they tell me. I was a little rundown. The labor was a little longer than I would have liked." She glossed over those awful moments when she had cried out his name over and over, sure that she was going to die. "When they brought the baby to me, one of the nurses said that she thought the name Keele was an unusual one for a baby, but that is what I had told them I was going to call a boy." D'Arcy soothed him when he moaned into her hair, feeling his pain.

"God, I should have been with you. You were so alone. You needed me." His voice cracked.

D'Arcy saw the moist gold of those eyes as he looked down at her. "I'll always need you. I need you now." She felt a boulder lift from her spirit. The sudden freedom gave her the feeling that she might float to the ceiling at any moment.

His mouth was on hers, the firm tenderness of his tongue branding her mouth, searching and finding her tongue. "You are mine, D'Arcy. Kiss me." His mouth latched to hers, coaxing hers to become part of him. "I love you, D'Arcy. I have since I saw you in the hallway of that hotel in London. I thought, 'that's what I want.' You told me you were married in that puritan way that you had—and I wanted to kill the guy for taking what was mine. Then I saw the way Alessio looked at you and knew that he hadn't a clue to the woman you were, the woman you still are." His hands strayed to the zipper at the back of her silk sheath. D'Arcy leaned forward to make it easier. He sighed as the dress fell forward into his hands, exposing the creamy swell of breasts. He took one rose tip into his mouth, sucking gently. "Are your breasts fuller already, love?" he murmured, lifting his head to look down at her, his one hand caressing the fullness.

"Yes, I think so, but not much." D'Arcy was having trouble breathing.

"Did you nurse Sean?" Keele couldn't seem to get enough of her breasts.

"Yes, for about five months," D'Arcy mumbled arching her neck so that he would continue to kiss her there as well.

"God, I'm jealous of him, my own son, that he had what I want and need for five months." Keele finished removing her bra and began rolling her panty hose from her body. "I used to have nightmares about Alessio making love to you, then sometimes I'd dream of you with other men. It was hell. For two years after you left me, I used to drink myself to sleep so I wouldn't dream."

She tightened her arms around him, wanting to drive the bogeys away.

"When I thought another man had made you pregnant and right after you returned to the States after leaving me, I went out and got so drunk, I couldn't stand. Some of the fishermen who knew me as a kid let me sleep on their boat. Yanos told me that I kept calling out to someone named D'Arcy." He kissed her knees, then looked up at her, smiling. "You remember, don't you?"

"Yes." D'Arcy felt aglow. "You did that the night we met. You kissed my knees and I almost fainted at your gentleness with me. To me, it was the first time, and that's how I always thought of it, that the night you made love to me was the first time that it had happened to me."

He scooped her up into his arms, looking down at her naked body with a grin of possession. "I feel so damn good."

"Me too." She let her hands rove through his hair as he took the stairs two at a time. "I love you, Keele, and you belong to me." She glared at him when he lowered her to the bed. "I'm Irish, you know, and they can be just as possessive as Greeks."

"I belong to you." He laughed. "I wouldn't have it any other way."

When he enfolded her to him, she forestalled him by placing one finger on his mouth. His brows lifted in question. "What is it, my love?"

"Do you remember when you gave me my ring, you told me that you had had it made for me?"

"Questions at a time like this, woman!" Keele groaned, burying his face in her neck. Then he lifted his head, a lopsided grin on his face. "I often wondered if you thought about that remark. I could have kicked myself for saying it."

D'Arcy let her fingers feather his jaw. "You didn't buy it for me in New York, did you?" She felt her heart pick up speed at the look in his eyes.

"As I've said before, you don't miss anything." He kissed her once, hard. "I ordered that ring for you the day after I met you in London. I knew then that I wanted to marry you."

"Darling." D'Arcy felt her eyes fill as she clutched him to her. "I knew I loved you that night too."

One evening in late winter as she lay cuddled in her husband's arms in front of the fireplace, she was nodding off to sleep comforted by the steady beat of Keele's heart.

"Did any of them mean anything to you, D'Arcy?" The words seemed yanked from his mouth.

Blinking, D'Arcy lifted her head to look at him. "What? Who?"

"Steve Linnett and the other men you saw while we were apart. Did any of them mean anything to you?" he asked, his voice hoarse. "I was so damn jealous of Steve I could have broken his neck."

D'Arcy straightened so that she could look him in the eye. "From the time you made love to me in London, there was no one else but you. Oh, I dated a few times, but I found it boring. Even worse than boring were the times that made me think of you," she crooned to him, running her fingers through his hair.

"I love you, D'Arcy. I'll always want you."

"That's the way I feel." She frowned at him for a moment. "Did your women mean a great deal to you?"

He pulled her down to him again, chuckling. "I had some 'arrangements' with women before and after you, but they had no meaning after I met you. I was just trying to forget you."

"How about Gerta Olsen? Elena Arfos? Marianne Bolle?" D'Arcy punched the names out.

Keele shrugged. "What about them? I transferred Gerta to a new division in the Carolinas. She's a smart woman but she was getting on my nerves. Elena is a nuisance but she is Gregor's daughter, so I have to put up with her. Marianne Bolle has shares in Athene Ltd. To me she is a bore but..." He shrugged again. "It's not good business to alienate the stockholders."

D'Arcy looked at her husband's lion eyes and saw the truth there. "I love you, Keele Petrakis, and I'm so happy you love me and my bulbous body."

"Don't say that about my beautiful wife," he muttered, pushing her back into the cushions and beginning to caress her.

The hot July morning Keele raced to the hospital, he was white-faced but calm. He stayed with her through the labor, helping her with her exercises, walking with her.

Katherine D'Arcy Petrakis was born with a minimum of fuss, flabbergasting her father with her beauty.

D'Arcy overflowed with love for him when she felt the moistness of his cheeks when he held her close to him. "I love our daughter, but you, my love, are my life, and when I saw your body clench in pain, I felt the pain and I knew there would never be a life for me without you."

D'Arcy felt his mouth on hers like a gentle covenant, as she stroked his stubbled cheeks and sighed in contentment.

Second Chance at Love

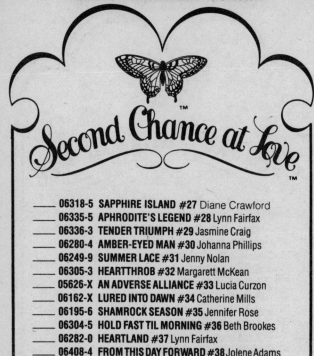

QUESTIONNAIRE

1. How many romances do you *read* each month? _____

2. How many of these do you *buy* each month? _____

3. Do you read primarily
   - ☐ novels in romance lines like SECOND CHANCE AT LOVE
   - ☐ historical romances
   - ☐ bestselling contemporary romances
   - ☐ other _____

4. Were the love scenes in this novel (this is book # _____)
   - ☐ too explicit
   - ☐ not explicit enough
   - ☐ tastefully handled

5. On what basis do you make your decision to buy a romance?
   - ☐ friend's recommendation
   - ☐ bookseller's recommendation
   - ☐ art on the front cover
   - ☐ description of the plot on the back cover
   - ☐ author
   - ☐ other _____

6. Where did you buy this book?
   - ☐ chain store (drug, department, etc.)
   - ☐ bookstore
   - ☐ supermarket
   - ☐ other _____

7. Mind telling your age?
   - ☐ under 18
   - ☐ 18 to 30
   - ☐ 31 to 45
   - ☐ over 45

8. How many SECOND CHANCE AT LOVE novels have you read?
   - ☐ this is the first
   - ☐ some (give number, please _____)

9. How do you rate SECOND CHANCE AT LOVE vs. competing lines?
   - ☐ poor
   - ☐ fair
   - ☐ good
   - ☐ excellent

10. Check here if you would like to
    - ☐ receive the SECOND CHANCE AT LOVE Newsletter

. . . .

Fill-in your name and address below:

name:_____

street address:_____

city_____ state_____ zip_____

Please share your other ideas about romances with us on an additional sheet and attach it securely to this questionnaire.

PLEASE RETURN THIS QUESTIONNAIRE TO:
SECOND CHANCE AT LOVE, THE BERKLEY/JOVE PUBLISHING GROUP
200 Madison Avenue, New York, New York 10016